Praise for
Kristine Kathryn Rusch

"Rusch is a great storyteller."

—*RT Book Reviews*

"Whether [Rusch] writes high fantasy, horror, sf, or contemporary fantasy, I've always been fascinated by her ability to tell a story with that enviable gift of invisible prose. She's one of those very few writers whose style takes me right into the story—the words and pages disappear as the characters and their story swallows me whole....Rusch has style."

—Charles de Lint

"A masterful writer is at work."

—Orson Scott Card
New York Times bestselling author

"Rusch's greatest strength...is her ability to close down a story and leave the reader feeling that the author could not possibly have wrung any more satisfaction out of the piece."

—*The Kansas City Star*

"Rusch is a great storyteller—easily the equal of Patterson or Koontz."

—*Analog*

Praise for the Smokey Dalton series
(writing as Kris Nelscott)

"Nelscott's series setting, in the turbulent late '60s, gives her books layers of issues of racism, class, and war, all of which still seem to remain sadly timely today."

—*Oregonian*

"Nelscott has her own, very distinct voice, and her series creates its own deeply satisfying pleasures and cogent points."

—*Seattle Times*

"Nelscott is good at conveying the edgy caution that blacks once brought to their movements among white society."

—*Houston Chronicle*

"(A) crime writer deliberately taking chances."

—*Chicago Tribune*

"It's not hard to draw parallels between Nelscott's PI Smokey Dalton and Walter Mosley's Easy Rawlins, another secretive, canny black man trying to solve mysteries while circumspectly navigating the white world. But Dalton's no knock-off. (Would you label the hundreds of hard-boiled detectives who've appeared in Raymond Chandler's wake mere Marlow Xeroxes because they're white?)"

—*Entertainment Weekly*

Also by
Kristine Kathryn Rusch

The Retrieval Artist Series:

The Disappeared
Extremes
Consequences
Buried Deep
Paloma
Recovery Man
Duplicate Effort
Anniversary Day
Blowback

The Smokey Dalton Series (as Kris Nelscott):

A Dangerous Road
Smoke-Filled Rooms
Thin Walls
Stone Cribs
War at Home
Days of Rage

Five Mystery Stories
Kristine Kathryn Rusch

wMG
Publishing

Five Mystery Stories

"The Moorhead House" by Kristine Kathryn Rusch first published in *Ellery Queen's Mystery Magazine*, January, 2008.

"Pudgygate" by Kristine Kathryn Rusch first published in *Cat Crimes Takes A Vacation*, edited by Ed Gorman & Martin H. Greenberg, Donald I. Fine, 1995.

"Scrawny Pete" by Kristine Kathryn Rusch first published as an Amazon Short, June 2005.

"Stomping Mad" by Kristine Kathryn Rusch first published in *Return of the Dinosaurs* edited by Mike Resnick and Martin H. Greenberg, Daw Books, 1997.

"G-Men" by Kristine Kathryn Rusch first published in *Sideways in Crime*, edited by Lou Anders, Solaris Books, 2008.

WMG Publishing
www.wmgpublishing.com

Contents

Five Mystery Stories
Kristine Kathryn Rusch

Introduction

UNTIL WMG PUBLISHING proposed putting my entire short fiction backlist online, I had no real idea why people called me a diverse writer. Sure, I write in a variety of genres. I even have not-so-secret identities for those genres, from Kris Nelscott for my historical mystery novels to Kristine Grayson for my paranormal romances, to good old Kristine Kathryn Rusch for my science fiction and fantasy.

I made a mistake back in 1989 when my short stories started appearing in major publications. On my short fiction, I kept the same byline. So Kristine Kathryn Rusch also writes short mystery fiction and short science fiction and short mainstream fiction—well, you get the idea.

And because I use the same name, I don't worry that much about genre. So when I started compiling the Rusch short stories, I was stunned to discover that my mystery stories hit almost every single mystery subgenre, and even twisted a few of those.

In this collection, you'll find "The Moorhead House," which is a *CSI*-type forensic mystery about a crime scene cleaner. "Pudgygate," a cozy, comes next, complete with a dinner party and a butler—and a cat. "Scrawny Pete," which also has a cat, is neither cozy nor forensic. It's a story of the mean streets; it's closer to noir than anything else.

"Stomping Mad" is another cozy, this one with an amateur detective who calls himself Spade, but who has a lot more in common with Nero Wolfe—if Nero Wolfe left his house and worked science fiction conventions.

And "G-Men" touches on science fiction as well, if only in its alternate history roots. "G-Men," which is, at heart, a political thriller combined with a police procedural, begins with a science-fiction what-if question: What if J. Edgar Hoover had died in 1964, a few years after John F. Kennedy.

"G-Men" appeared in several years' best collections, including *The Year's Best Science Fiction* and *The Best American Mystery Stories*, proving that genre is in the eye of the beholder.

I hope you will behold enough mystery here to intrigue you, and enough strangeness to get you to venture into some of my other favorite genres.

—*Kristine Kathryn Rusch*
Lincoln City, Oregon
July 26, 2010

The Moorhead House

THE HOUSE ON THE HILL had Christmas lights.

I stopped beside my van—white, with *DUSTY'S CLEANING* lettered in discreet gold. The van was camouflage—official enough, without advertising the kind of work I actually did—but people knew anyway. Hard to miss when the guy down the street offs himself, and a woman in a hazard suit, driving a van loaded with cleaning supplies, shows up a few days later.

But that day, I was alone. I was touring a cleaned scene, making sure my team had gotten every last bit. I wore my coveralls, a mask and three pairs of gloves, but I hadn't gone for the full treatment, thinking it unnecessary.

The neighborhood was solidly Oregon middle-class: old Victorians, 1930s bungalows, a few ranches; late-model cars, all probably bought on time; and lovely yards with only a little grass and lots of perennials. The kind of neighborhood a prospective buyer would look at and think of as a nice place to raise kids, the kind of place you grow old in, where your neighbors watch out for you, and keep track of every little thing.

But I'd been here four times in the ten years I'd owned this business—for the Hansen suicide (right in the living room, where the kids couldn't miss it. Bastard); the Palmer home-invasion-gone-wrong (the crime scene techs had missed the cat, curled up under the stove where it had apparently crawled to nurse its wounds); the well-known Bransted murder (the little girl had been dragged into a nearby garage and gutted there, mercifully after death); and the Moorhead ritual slaughter in the Victorian up the hill.

At least, the authorities believed it was a ritual slaughter. They never did find the bodies, although that place had four different high velocity spatters, and all sorts of ritualistic items—knives, black candles, destroyed crosses. That was the only case I'd ever been called to testify in, mostly because the members of that cult were convicted even though no one ever found the victims.

The murders had occurred over Christmas.

The first time I'd seen the Moorhead House, it'd been covered with Christmas lights like something out of a Hallmark greeting. All it needed had been two feet of snow, and a few carolers out front, holding their lanterns, their red-cheek faces upturned in wholesome rapturous praise.

My first partner'd quit after that job. Not that I blamed her. The Moorhead job had left me shaken too, and I'm not the shakable type. I'm a former firefighter and EMT, one of the first women in the state to do that kind of work, and I've battled both flame and discrimination with equal ferocity. I've seen what people can do to each other, and I've learned to accept it most of the time.

Since then, the Moorhead House had sold more than once, but no one had ever been able to live there long. So far as I knew, the place had been empty for years.

The Christmas lights bothered me.

They were up in the same place those original lights had been, white icicles—popular ten years ago—dripping down like melted frosting off the gables and the eaves of the Queen Anne.

So much like that dusky winter afternoon, when I'd seen the destruction for the first time.

Back then, I had no clue how to handle the destruction, the tears that cleaning a drop of blood from the back of a lamp might bring. I tried to pretend that I was just cleaning a place, a very filthy place, and I was beginning to realize that would never really function, that you couldn't stop the brain from wondering how it must've felt among the screams and the crashing and the glinting knife.

The state waited nearly a month before letting us in. By then, the place smelled like ancient rot and old blood.

That smell came back to me as I stared at those lights, promising a festive afternoon to anyone who would just march up the hill, and knock.

***

"Who's in the Moorhead House?" I asked when I got back to the office. "Office" is too big a word for the place: that makes it sound like we all have desks and secretaries and official nameplates. In reality, I have a tiny office and the rest of the place is two rooms—the front area with a desk, a phone, and a Coke machine that Debbie insisted on as well as a warehouse-style back room, filled with all manner of cleaning equipment, industrial strength showers, and five commercial washer and dryer sets.

Marcus sat behind the desk that afternoon. He's a big guy with a deep, reassuring voice, the kind folks like to hear when they've had a death in the family and decide to hire us themselves.

"Seen the lights, huh?" he said, leaning back in his chair and folding his massive hands over his surprisingly flat stomach.

"Yeah." I punched the Coke machine, and a root beer fell out.

We'd long ago bought the cola people out, filled the machine with our favorite cans, and shut off the payment mechanism. Now the thing works like an oversized (and expensive) refrigerator. I don't get rid of it though, because it's the only nifty part of our office.

"To be honest," I said, popping the top, "it scared me a little."

"Dwayne said that too."

I'd forgotten Dwayne worked the second part of that job—when the first set of new owners somehow got it into their heads that the tiny bones in the septic system belonged to the murdered family. The bones actually belonged to a family of squirrels. But by then, the crime scene techs had been back to the house and the lawn dug up. The mess was incredible, and the crime scene people decided to call us.

Not that it mattered to the first new owners. They sold as soon as the place was presentable again.

"How come that job weirded you out?" Marcus asked.

I shrugged, took a sip of the root beer, and said, "Sometimes I wonder why more jobs don't weird me out."

"Nice avoidance," he said. "Now answer."

I smiled at him. "Because there're no bodies."

"There're never any bodies when we go in," he said.

Which wasn't entirely true. There was that cat in the Palmer house and farther downtown, a stray dog left on the back porch. One of our other cleaning teams discovered an infant in a back closet, an infant which hadn't been part of the murder that the team had been cleaning up.

But I got Marcus's point. The bodies that we cleaned up after were long gone by the time we got to the house. We always knew what happened—we had to, so that we would know where to look for debris or spatter or pieces of skin—but we almost never saw the corpse.

"I think it would have been easier if there had been bodies." I set the root beer down. "It was the uncertainty."

Or maybe it had been my uncertainty. As an EMT, I'd pulled dying people out of car wrecks. As a firefighter, I'd been at houses where the children didn't get out, where the remaining person on the fifth floor refused to jump, where entire families died in their sleep.

But nothing prepared me for the emptiness of a crime scene. The moved furniture, the ruined rugs, the destroyed curtains. The toys that were pushed against the wall, the broken vases, the shattered lamps.

We couldn't repair that stuff. Our mission was to make sure no one could tell a violent or neglected death had happened in this place. And if the family still lived there, our mission was to make the place look like it had before what we euphemistically called, "The Event."

But the Moorhead House was the first place I worked without a family to move back into it or without an owner overseeing the job we did on the rental property.

No family left, no extended family leaving messages on my machine, no potential owners waiting to rebuild the place according to their new vision.

I tried not to look at the Moorhead House as I drove to my next job. It wasn't far away—another suicide, damn the holiday season—and from the back door of a kitchen that hadn't been cleaned since 1978, I could see the lights of the Moorhead House against the rain-darkened sky.

I tried to ignore it, to concentrate on the life lost, the loneliness that seemed to be the cause. This man hadn't been found for nearly two weeks, which put his death on Thanksgiving Day. The remains of a small turkey and the store-bought pumpkin pie confirmed that.

He had family—an estranged wife who hadn't seen him in nearly thirty years, two children now grown, and parents who sounded genuinely hurt when they hired us over the phone.

I'd learned, though, that genuine hurt sometimes sounded brusque or businesslike, not thick with tears.

And I wondered about a man whose house was so dirty that the neighbors didn't complain about the odor because they were used to odors coming from the place.

I never told my co-workers that I thought about the dead as if I were the last person who would remember them. Sometimes, perhaps, I was. Certainly the family of that man wouldn't know how bleak his life was at the end. Even if one of us told them, they wouldn't be able to imagine the piled up papers, the half-written letters, the battered but comfortable chair in front of the TV.

I recognized this house because it was a filthy version of my own.

My place is spotless. Because my hours are long and my moods uncertain, I don't keep a pet. I have the battered but comfortable single chair in front of a too-big television, only it's in my basement, not the center of the living room.

If someone asked me, I'd never admit to being lonely.

Usually I don't mind.

Except on difficult days, days when I'm cleaning out someone else's solitary home.

***

THE INVITATION CAME TWO DAYS LATER. The city's annual bash, held for the contractors and private firms that kept the city running, was always a big deal. The planners spared no expense. Once they rented a yacht to follow the old ferry route across the river. Another time, they commandeered the largest, trendiest nightclub in the city. And one time—the only time (because too many people complained)—they held a beautiful secular service at the city's historic Presbyterian Church.

This year, however. This year's site was a stunner.

Debbie handed me the invite not three minutes after the mail arrived. I was sitting in my office, enjoying a rare moment of quiet. I had that week's checks spread in front of me. I was thinking about the bank deposit, and having a healthy bank balance at the Christmas holidays for the first time since I'd opened the business.

"Boss," Debbie said.

I looked up. Her normally dusky skin had paled to an abnormal gray color. She held the invitation between her thumb and forefinger as if it smelled bad.

It didn't look bad. In fact, I recognized it. We usually didn't get formal invitations here, not the kind with the gold foil borders and the hand calligraphy.

"What's wrong?" I asked.

She handed me the invite. It was on a stiff cardboard stock that felt like expensive parchment. I glanced at the language, familiar with it after ten years of parties.

"The annual party," I said. "So?"

"Look where they're holding it."

I did. And felt the blood leave my face as well.

The Moorhead House.

"Get me the envelope," I said.

She went back to reception. I could see her through my door, rummaging through the wastebasket. When she finally found the envelope, she carried it back to me in the same way she had carried the invite itself—thumb and forefinger, as if the entire thing would infect her.

I took the envelope from her. It was made of a matching stock and had a metered city hall postmark from the day before. If someone had sent this as a joke, they would have had to duplicate the card stock and use the city hall postage meter, which gets guarded like crazy so that city hall employees don't use it for personal letters.

"Crap," I said, and reached for the phone.

I dialed the RSVP number at the bottom of the invite. After a few rings, I got the voice mail of a person I didn't know. I hung up, and dialed the deputy mayor, Greg Raabe. We had gone to college together. We'd even dated a few times before I had found my calling and before he had met his wife.

His secretary picked up immediately, and when she heard it was me, put me through even faster.

"Greg," I said without preamble, "what's this about the Christmas party at the Moorhead House? Do you remember what happened there?"

"I remember," he said, which was not the response I expected. I expected some political dance or an actual lapse of memory. The fact that he answered—and sounded disgusted—meant that he had fielded more than one call about this.

"Don't you think this is a little inappropriate?"

"What I think doesn't matter," he said. "It's a done deal."

"Why?" I asked.

"Because," he said, "the city bought the building. They plan to turn it into a museum."

***

THAT WAS THE THING about the Moorhead House, the thing no one talked about any more. Shortly after the family died, the National Register of Historic Places placed the house on its registry. Apparently someone had gone through the entire historic preservation rigmarole in the years before the murders.

Fortunately for me, the certification came after we cleaned the place up. If it had come before, the job would have taken much longer, and the city would have been billed for a great deal more money.

Historic preservation crime scene cleaning required an entirely different use of chemicals, several kinds of oversight, and all sorts of paperwork, things I'd just managed to avoid.

I'd managed to overlook most of that and had, in fact, forgotten it, until Greg Raabe had said the word "museum."

The Moorhead House had been the first home built on this side of the river. The fabulously wealthy Moorheads had made their money in various enterprises in the Oregon territory, from logging to mining to trading supplies. Then they bought up the land surrounding the river, and sold it, piecemeal, to settlers coming down the Oregon Trail.

The Moorheads kept large portions of the land, however, much of it near the river, so that they could control the ferries (the only way to get across and head to Portland, even then the state's major city). The river also gave them added control of the logging industry. In those days, logs floated down the river to be collected at sloughs which were also owned by the Moorheads. Over time, the river land became a center for what little industry the city had, and the rents made the Moorheads even wealthier.

But they became enchanted with their wealth, and wanted a lot more power than owning a single small city would give them. The great-grandsons of the original family moved to Portland, where they bought even grander houses on even grander hills. Their sons became politicians, and their children became drug-addicted deadbeats who had every privilege.

Somewhere along the way, the holdings here got sold. Then the houses in Portland went, and finally, the famous family, now down to an infamous few, had only enough left to maintain their townhouses in Washington D.C.

The Moorhead House, symbol of the wealth and power of a bygone age, had—even before the federal government decided to protect it—become the symbol of death and destruction in the modern age.

"A museum?" I asked.

"People love a mystery," Greg said in that dryly bland voice, the one I always thought of as his political voice.

"And the house is truly historical. The museum will have one room dedicated to the murders, but it'll be upstairs. The rest'll talk about city history, the impact of the Moorheads, and the way that this part of Oregon once seemed like the center of the universe."

Then I knew he was being sarcastic. He never used that phrase in serious conversation.

"Whose idea was this?" I asked.

"You read about it in the papers?" he asked as if that was an answer.

"No," I said.

"Then think about it."

I did, and it only took me a minute to understand. The mayor had done this. The mayor, Louise Vogel, had set herself up as a minor dictator, much to the disgust of everyone outside of her party and even some within.

She had the benefit of being one of the few people in the city who would take the job, which paid next to nothing for the amount of work it took. Greg had become deputy mayor as a sort of oversight position, but she had defanged him quickly. She owned much of the council, bought, I was told, with a combination of blood money and blackmail threats. The woman knew how to run small city politics.

"Why in the world would Louise want the Moorhead House as a museum?" I asked.

"I have no idea," Greg said. "Makes as much sense to me as holding a Christmas party there. So, are you coming?"

"I cleaned the place, Greg," I said softly. "I had to testify at the trial."

"Oh." He was silent for a moment. Then he sighed. "I'm supposed to jolly people into attending."

"Has it been working?"

"So far," he said. "Apparently, people like to pretend they're not interested in death houses, but they really are."

Unless they see the houses in full aftermath.

"I suppose it'll be a grand affair," I said, mimicking his dry voice.

"It'll be memorable, that's for sure," he said, and signed off.

I held onto the phone for a moment longer, mostly to fend off Debbie's questions. As she listened to my conversation, she seemed to have gotten ahold of herself. She shook her head and shifted from foot to foot, as if she could barely contain herself.

I set the receiver down. "It's no joke."

She swallowed. "Are we going?"

The city's party was always the highlight of our year.

"Greg says the party'll be memorable," I said.

"People will talk about it for a long time," she said.

I adjusted some of the checks in front of me. My pleasure in my unusual wealth at year's end had faded.

"Let's make attendance optional this year," I said. "And before anyone agrees to go, make sure they know that the party'll be at Moorhead House."

"Okay." Debbie started to leave my office, then she paused at the door. "You going?"

"I don't know," I said, and realized, to my surprise, that I had just spoken the truth.

***

I SUPPOSE, POLITICALLY, I should have said I was going to go. My job, after all, was to make buildings habitable again. Part of habitable was holding festive events—weddings, bar mitzvahs, Christmas parties.

But habitable was different than comfortable. And habitable wasn't always possible.

Places like Moorhead House were notorious, and notoriety lingered long after the physical examples of the crimes had disappeared.

In the end, it was my curiosity that took me there. I wanted to see the house in all its glory. I wanted to know if it could still have glory.

And I wanted to know exactly what Louise Vogel was up to this time.

***

NO ONE ELSE FROM THE OFFICE wanted to go. Debbie actually called me ghoulish, even though I wasn't the person holding the party. Dwayne looked at me with pity, asked me if I was sure, and when I said I was, he visibly shuddered. Then he told me, quietly, that he'd never go in that house again, not even if I paid him to do so.

In the end, Marcus went with me, mostly because he was curious. He'd been hired long after I did the first part of the Moorhead House job, but he was there for the tail end of the trial, and for Dwayne's run at the tiny bones in the sewers. Marcus told me he'd always wanted to go inside, and acknowledged that it was an unhealthy curiosity, based as much on the missing bodies as it was on the effect the entire place had had on our office.

He picked me up at eight. I'd forgotten how well he cleaned up. He wore a long jacket over dress pants—a modern suit that harked back to the Old West—and instead of looking like a football player stuffed into his younger brother's clothing, he looked like something out of *GQ*.

I felt dowdy in comparison. I wore a black velvet dress, and I decked it with a red scarf and some glittery (but fake) jewelry I'd inherited from my great aunt. My matching black velvet heels required, of all things, dusting, and I had to run out an hour before the party to buy panty hose without runs or pulls.

Marcus waited inside my foyer while I dithered over coats and purses, feeling more like a girl-girl than I had for awhile. Once upon a time, I had cared about things like make-up and matching purses with shoes, but I had lost that at nineteen, when I'd come home from college to find my mother dead of a stroke on the kitchen floor.

She had been there for a week. My parents were divorced—my father lived in another state—and I was an only child. I had come home to surprise my mother, and instead, she had surprised me.

Marcus had a 1960s Mustang that he took out for special occasions, and apparently this ranked as one of those. He drove to the Moorhead House in silence. Normally, we would have chattered the entire way—Marcus and I share the same taste in movies, books, and politics—but those subjects paled in comparison to the house.

The Mustang rode lower than my van, so the view of the Moorhead House as we turned onto the street below seemed even more impressive that usual. This close to Christmas, you'd think other homes on the block would have decorations on the windows or lights strung outside, but the Moorhead House seemed to be the only one with Christmas spirit.

I looked up at the place as we started toward the drive, and those icicle lights still sent a chill through me. I almost told Marcus to turn around and I'd buy him dinner at a nearby steakhouse so we wouldn't waste the dress-up clothes, but I didn't. I knew better than to seem weak in front of one of my employees.

I'd learned that lesson as a female fire-fighter. Even when you felt uncomfortable, you took a deep breath and went into the smoke. To do anything less meant you couldn't perform your duties.

And somehow, this party had become one of my duties.

***

WE WERE ARRIVING DELIBERATELY LATE. I hated showing up early to any party. Marcus pulled the Mustang into the circular drive, and my breath caught.

Some things were different: the hedges had been clipped to the bone and did not have lights hanging from them as they had that murderous Christmas season. Signs had been planted in what had been the yard but was now obviously going to be a garden, warning guests to stay on the paths. The signs had been hand-calligraphed, and looked expensive. They even had little drawings of holly around the edges.

I hated them.

Marcus looked at me as he got out of the Mustang, and then he grinned like a little boy who was about to do something wrong.

"Ready, boss?" he asked.

I'd never be ready, but I smiled gamely and put my hand on his massive arm. He helped me pick my way across the path. The air was cold and damp, but the pine boughs near the house gave off a Christmasy scent that I hadn't expected.

Suddenly I felt younger than I had in years, almost like that girl I'd left in my mother's kitchen, and my heart lifted. A party was just what I needed. If I could forget the house, or at least look on its new role as host as a personal victory, I might be able to have a good time.

We stepped onto the porch together. Inside the frosted glass windows, we could see shapes moving against yellow light.

My stomach clenched, and I swallowed convulsively. I wasn't sure I could do this.

Marcus gave me a sideways glance. "You okay?"

I nodded because I couldn't answer. He knocked on the door.

Someone pulled it open and the smells of burning wood and baking cookies filled the air. Laughter came along with Mel Torme's voice, singing about Jack Frost nipping at noses. The man who opened the door had a Santa hat over graying hair. The hat didn't go with his exquisitely tailored suit.

He held a glass clearly filled with eggnog in one hand. With the other, he gestured toward the interior. "Merry, merry!"

"Happy, happy," Marcus said, making fun of him.

But the man didn't seem to notice. He clapped Marcus on the back as we walked inside.

The place was transformed. If I hadn't known it was the house in which I'd spent a week cleaning, I wouldn't have recognized it. To my right, the curved staircase was once again the center of the house. Someone had wrapped garlands of holly around the mahogany banister, probably with no thought to how old, how rare or how valuable the wood was.

People stood on the stairs, holding drinks, talking, some looking at the portraits hung over the stairs, others heading up to see what else the house had in store.

Coats were piled on top of the telephone seat built against the wall. The carpets were gone, revealing wood floors that matched the wood trim throughout the house.

I couldn't imagine what it had cost to clean the floors. I had cleaned the carpets and recommended their removal, but no one had done that—at least not for the first family which bought the place. I had warned the realtors that if anyone took up the carpets, they might find horrible stains beneath. I had removed the rugs myself in the upstairs bedroom where two of the family members had bled to death (there was no saving those rugs, and no attempt to), but the ones down here had had bloody footprints and drag marks, and other stains that I never could quite identify.

"You're staring," Marcus whispered.

At least, I thought he whispered it, although he might have spoken in a normal tone. The party noises going on around us made it hard to hear much more than the rumble of conversation. The music was classy and so were the people around me. Hard to believe most of them spent their days in jeans and overalls or uniforms paid for by the city.

"Sorry," I whispered.

"Is it different?" he asked.

"Yeah."

I led Marcus into what had once been the front parlor. The pocket doors were gone, along with most of the walls that contained them, so now the front and back parlors were one room (with an arch) that modern people would call the living room.

The furniture was fake period with a fainting couch, a regular couch, and overstuffed armchairs. Too many tables crowded the bay window, and on those tables stood food of all sorts from cookies and sliced pies to small unidentifiable appetizers and toothpicked bits of fruit and cheese.

Marcus grabbed a small plate, shaking it with surprise. "China."

"Nothing but the best," I muttered, and doubted he could hear me.

I couldn't eat, even if I wanted to. I left him there, debating whether to have strawberries dipped in chocolate or chocolate-covered cherry truffles. From a passing waiter carrying a tray of beverages on his outstretched palm, I snatched a flute of champagne, carrying it with me as I went from room to room.

The place had clearly been professionally decorated. From the furniture to the draped pine boughs and hanging mistletoe, the interior looked like something out of *House Beautiful*.

The Christmas tree, at the far wall of what had been the back parlor, took up so much space that it seemed to be growing out of the floor. It was decorated in silver bows, tinsel, and little silver lights that blinked on and off. An embarrassing display of packages hid the lower branches.

I knew from previous parties that the packages would be gone by the night's end, a mound of paper left for someone else to clean up, and the gifts would seem less impressive unwrapped than they did at this moment.

A *Do-Not-Enter* sign had been taped to the swinging kitchen door, the only infelicity in the entire place. I ignored it, and went inside anyway, drawn by the smells of baking cookies. Small women in rented tuxedos and looking hot, wiped hair away from their faces. Two coaxed a stainless steel dishwasher to take more dishes. Another woman bent over the stove, and yet another was placing crudités on a silver tray.

Men, as tall as the women were small, picked up the trays. The men also wore tuxes, but on them, the tuxes looked natural. Maybe because they were in traditional serving roles, where the women, stuck in the kitchen, should have been in simple black dresses with aprons to complete the servant illusion.

"You're not supposed to be here," said the woman filling the trays.

"That's all right," I said. "I used to work here."

One of the men looked at me sharply. He frowned a little, as if wondering how anyone could have worked here, given the history of the house. Or maybe I was reading too much into a slight reaction. Maybe he thought my lame excuse for being in the kitchen was just that. I smiled at him, and slipped out of the way.

The kitchen was dramatically different, remodeled about the time of the bones discovered in the sewer drain. The stove was restaurant quality, the refrigerator one of those stainless steel subzero monstrosities that looked like it could eat an entire room.

Everything was different, and somehow I found that more disconcerting than the Christmas decorations around front. When I had cleaned this place, the kitchen had been my haven—the only room without much blood in the entire house, and that blood only came from the detectives and crime scene techs. Harmless, innocuous drops, left by people who were trying to solve the crime, not the people who had created it.

My stomach was churning. The smell of food was making me ill. I pushed open the swinging door and stepped back into the living room.

Marcus was talking to a pretty woman in a slinky blue dress. Louise was standing near the tree, gesturing at the presents. She looked even thinner than usual, her face bony, her black hair pulled into a tight bun.

Her gaze caught mine, flat and challenging. I lifted my still full glass in a silent toast. She smiled—a real and warm smile, something I had never seen from her before—and raised her glass as well. We drank in concert from separate parts of the room as if we were old friends.

"I see you've kissed and made up." Greg Raabe, the deputy mayor who had told me about this debacle, had sidled up beside me. He knew how much I disliked Louise, and how that feeling seemed to be mutual.

I turned to him and smiled. He no longer looked like the boy I'd dated in school. That boy had been reedy slender and blond, with no muscles at all. His bright blue eyes had dominated his face.

The eyes remained the same, dominating and filled with personality, but the rest of him had changed. He was as heavy as he had once been slight, and in place of those visible ribs were rock-hard abs from all the weights he lifted. He ate to compensate for the tension, I think, because he didn't drink or smoke, and to compensate for the eating, he exercised.

"There was no kissing," I said to him, happier than I wanted to be to see him. "I just saluted her, that's all. This is quite the party."

"This is quite the expense," he said. "Imagine what the council will say when they see this on the city budget."

I grinned. "Fortunately, that's not my job."

"But it could be mine," he said, looking at her talking to the man near the presents. "I was kind of hoping that once she had her stepping stone to the governorship, I could become mayor."

"One party won't get in the way," I said.

"You're assuming that this party is the only budget item that'll bother them." He sighed and grabbed his own champagne flute from a passing waiter.

I looked up at the waiter as he went by. It was the man who had frowned in the kitchen. He looked familiar. His skin was a ruddy color that wasn't common in the Pacific Northwest, except among people who worked on the ocean. He had a square jaw, and hard cheekbones, the kind I always associated with those 1930s pictures of Aryan youth.

"Know him?" Greg asked.

"He looks familiar," I said as he went into the kitchen. "Does he to you?"

"In a generic waiterly way." Greg smiled. "I told Louise we should have dancing, but she didn't listen to me."

"There's no room," I said. Besides, Greg wouldn't have been able to dance with me even if there had been music.

His wife Emma pretended that the fact we dated didn't bother her, when, in fact, it was very clear that it did.

I scanned the room, but didn't see her. "Is Emma upstairs?"

The smile left his face. "She wouldn't come."

"Because of the house?" I asked.

"Because of the separation." His voice was low. "She doesn't like my ambitions."

Emma had always wanted Greg to settle down and make money. He had always been more interested in public service than in making monetary use of his expensive law degree. Apparently the fights had come to a head.

"When did you separate?" I asked.

He shushed me and whispered. "Not everyone knows."

"Sorry," I said.

"It happened last week. I have an apartment near city hall, which I'd had anyway. I guess I knew this was coming."

Everyone had known this was coming, maybe even from the moment the vows were taken. But Greg seemed quietly devastated.

I put my hand on his shoulder, startled to feel the same kind of muscles I had felt on Marcus. "I'm really sorry," I said again.

Greg grinned. The look didn't quite meet his eyes. "No, you're not. You never liked Emma."

Not many of his friends had, and I always figured the ones who had liked her just pretended for Greg's sake.

"I am sorry," I said. "For you. This is hard."

"Yeah," he said, and then sighed. "Duty beckons."

Duty didn't, but Louise did. She was waving him over with a hand so manicured I could see the shine of the nail polish from here. Time for the packages. I hoped they got to my name quickly. I was ready to leave.

Marcus had left his new conquest and came over beside me. "Did you check the upstairs?"

I shook my head. I hadn't forgotten the upstairs, but I didn't see the need to torture myself. "I ducked into the kitchen for a while."

Which reminded me of the waiter, whom I no longer saw. "Did you notice that waiter, the one who looked like he'd been a member of the Hitler Youth?"

"No," Marcus said. "Why?"

Greg had clapped his hands for quiet. I sighed. I knew this drill. First they'd demand silence, then they'd hand out gifts. Louise worked off a list. I had noted last year that the city contractors like me got one of two things: an espresso maker (if the city had spent a lot of money on you) or a care basket filled with all kinds of city products, like salmon and some of our famous cheese and locally grown filberts.

I, of course, had gotten a care basket, even though the city spent a lot of money on our services. I thought that it was merely an oversight, then Greg had reminded me that we weren't listed in the budget. We were buried in other line items. So no one really knew how much money we made cleaning up local property except maybe Debbie and me.

Greg started calling out names. The man beside Louise handed out the packages, and Louise kept charge of the list. People walked up, got large gaudily wrapped gifts, and then walked away, grinning.

Marcus rolled his eyes. "How long is this going to take?"

"Usually about an hour," I said. "You want to go back and make goo-goo eyes at that sweet young thing?"

"She's hard to talk to," he said.

"Because?" I asked.

His face shut down. "Because I told her what I do."

That was one of the major drawbacks to our business. People thought we were on the level of grave diggers and morticians. Even the popularity of programs like *CSI*, which made one small aspect of death work glamorous, didn't spill over to us.

"Tough break," I said.

He shrugged. "Anyone with reactions like that's too shallow for me."

But he didn't sound sincere. And then he took my champagne and finished it for me. I watched him drink another, and decided that at some point in the evening, I'd have to wrestle the Mustang's keys from him, and get us home.

***

IT TOOK TWO MORE HOURS before we could leave. I never did see the waiter again, but I got absorbed in my present—a small wireless weather forecasting kit, with barometer and thermometer, something that actually appealed to my scientific sensibilities. Marcus slowed on the drinks—he'd found another pretty woman to chat up, and apparently this time, he didn't make the mistake of telling her what he did—and I didn't want to interrupt his rhythm.

I looked at the stairs twice, but I didn't go up them. I searched for Greg, and found Louise instead. She was leaning against a side of the arch, holding but not drinking a glass of champagne. She watched the proceeding with tired eyes.

When she saw me, she smiled again.

I wasn't sure I liked that. Two real smiles from Louise in one evening. Something had to be wrong.

"It's going well, isn't it?" she asked.

"Better than I would have thought," I said.

She sipped the champagne—or pretended to. Maybe that was one of her secrets. Pretending to drink when everyone around her got blotto.

"It's a tribute to you people," she said.

At first, I thought she meant the little people, the non-politicos, and then I realized she actually meant us, Dusty's Cleaning.

"Thanks," I said, glancing at those stairs.

"I mean it," she said. "This place is cheerful. Who would have thought?"

I looked at her. Her entire face looked tired, and she was too thin. Maybe it was the strain of the party, or maybe something else had gone wrong in her life. I wasn't sure, and I wasn't about to ask.

"It's what we do," I said.

"Exorcise the ghosts," she said, as if in agreement.

But the ghosts weren't exorcised for me. They still lurked beneath the party favors and the seasonal joy. When this crowd left, and the caterers finished, when the last staff member shut off the lights, the house would revert to its post-murder self. The high-velocity spatter would paint itself on the walls, the cries would echo in the upstairs bedroom, and the blood would seep into the rugs.

I shuddered. I couldn't help it.

Of course, Louise noticed. "Does it still bother you?"

"Sometimes," I said before I could stop myself, "I think places like this should be burned."

Louise frowned at me. "That's an odd sentiment, coming from you."

I shrugged. "There are some places," I said, "that never get entirely clean."

***

THE DREAM CAME AS IT OFTEN DID. It started with my mother. She was on the floor of our kitchen, the smell of Lemon Pledge filling the air. When she saw me, she stood, apologized, and offered to cook. I thought it inappropriate to have the newly dead make the meal, and I told her so, even though I knew I was disappointing her.

She slipped out the side door, and as she did, she said, "You'll never see me again."

Only as I mulled the words, I realized she hadn't said "see," she had said "find." *You'll never find me again.*

Then, in the transitionless magic of dreams, I stood in the foyer of the Moorhead House. The place smelled of weeks-old blood and voided bowels. Beneath those smells was that of rotted flesh.

As I stood there, I existed on two levels: the woman standing in the foyer, and the woman who knew every inch of that house, the one who had cleaned it all and who would, if she wasn't careful, become obsessed with it.

The walls in the upstairs bedroom had a spatter pattern that looked like a post-modernist painting. I knew that it was spray—a knife or something sharp pierced an artery, and the blood sprayed before the dying man? woman? child? turned so that the rest of the blood would shoot against a different wall.

Then the dream changed. The waiter stared at me with those cold blue eyes. I'd seen them before. Not at a party where he was curiously out of place but at the trial.

He sat in the second row from the back, and watched my every move. His face wasn't ruddy then, but he was thinner, sadder, and his eyes had fear in them.

I couldn't look at him as I testified. He made me nervous.

That day, everyone made me nervous.

I thought nothing of it.

You'll never find me again.

Then the scene changed once more. My mother's kitchen, without her body lying on the middle of the floor, looked like a happy place—painted yellow, spotlessly clean. Only a chair had moved, tilted away from the table, as if its occupant left suddenly.

Add the body to the picture, sprawled along the tile, arms thrown backward, fluids staining the clothes, and the moved chair was ominous. Had she stood because she felt ill? Or had she simply been crossing to the refrigerator when her body gave out?

Or had she been laying there, helpless, only able to slide a chair a little toward her, thinking maybe it would help her up, but the experiment didn't work, and she remained—alone—on her back, until she breathed her last.

I sat up, not sure exactly when I woke, when the dream ended and the thinking began.

We could guess about the bodies in the Moorhead House, but we didn't know. We didn't know if the ritual items—the desecrated religious symbols, the black candles, the knives—had been added later to throw us off. Because they had been removed as evidence before I arrived, I didn't even know if they'd been covered with spatter, proving they'd been in position before the family died.

I did know that they left no impression wherever they'd been. There were no knife-sized holes in the spatter pattern, no black candle wax on the side tables.

Only the blood and the stink and the sense that something horrible had happened here.

I turned on my too-large television. One of the get-rich-quick real estate gurus hawked his no-money down method. As house after house flashed on the screen, I wondered what secrets those houses held.

Over time, the secrets faded.

All bodies disappeared, forgotten, lost.

Did the people who owned my mother's house now enjoy their kitchen? Did they walk easily over the spot where she had spent her last hours? Did they wonder how long her body had been there, waiting for someone to find her?

More importantly, did they care?

And that's when my stomach turned, when the crazy food that I had eaten backed up into my throat.

No one had cared at the Moorhead House party. If the murders were mentioned, it was with a salacious edge, as if the deaths were part of a setting, added for the party-goers' enjoyment.

Five people were missing, presumed dead—presumed because no one lost that much blood and lived.

But the police hadn't tested every drop. Only a few to make DNA comparisons, enough to build a case without a body—one of the toughest murder cases to bring. The cult, arrested, charged, and pulled off the street for life, had continually maintained their innocence.

I hadn't been able to look at them either when I testified—malnourished, scared twenty-somethings who'd used too many drugs and lived too close to the crime scene.

People had seen them in the house, but no one had seen them on the night of the murders.

No one had seen anything that night, even though the house dominated that hillside.

Even though the house dominated the entire town.

***

THE NEXT MORNING, we had a fire-clean. Mostly smoke and water damage. The apartment, on the lower floor of a large complex, had lost its kitchen, and the rest was ruined. But the upper floors were still livable if we could get the stench out, which we could.

The apartments had been evacuated, but they still held the stuff of people's lives—dolls scattered on a bedroom floor, slippers kicked aside in someone's haste to escape, a half-eaten pizza on a scarred coffee table.

I surveyed the damage, realized the cleaning would be one of our easier jobs, and called in a junior team. Then I went back to the office, and pulled the Moorhead files.

The image of my mother's kitchen chair, fresh from my dream, haunted me. We had approached the Moorhead scene with a single assumption: that the family had been slaughtered there in a ritualistic way, and the bodies had then been moved.

But what if there had been no ritual? What if this had been a crime of passion? Blood was everywhere in that house, except the kitchen, an oddity explained at the time by the ritualistic nature of the deaths.

I didn't have crime scene photos, but I did have my photos of the scene. It was the early days of my business; I did before-and-after photos for prospective clients.

The before photos were vicious and dark, grimmer than I remembered. But the blood spatter, the filth left from violent death, was much as my memory held it—a long, continuous spray, followed by real spatter, arcing as the blood pulsed from someone's body.

In one photo, my hand pressed on the rug, releasing the blood contained within. In another, the rivulets of blood went down the stairs, drops alongside heading away from the scene.

What had the police tested? What had they ignored?

I thumbed through until I found the bathrooms. They, like the bedrooms, were thick with blood. The toilet, the bathtub, and the sinks had light spray, but nothing inside the porcelain basins, suggesting that no one had cleaned up there.

No one had cleaned in the kitchen either.

I stared at the images, trying to recall the lesson of the dream. Take away my expectations, and what did I see?

A charnel house.

A place where blood was allowed to flow freely and for some time.

I closed the file and leaned on it, my stomach as queasy as it had been the night before. I rubbed my eyes, sighed heavily, and picked up the phone.

**

I HAD A LOT OF CONTACTS at the police department. Early on, they had considered me part of the brotherhood, mostly because of my EMT and fire training, and they handed out my cards to grieving widows and distraught adult children.

Over time, several officers would call me before the city did, letting me know I had a job on the way, and preparing me, so that I could put the proper team on it. If the case was sensitive, I often did the work myself. That way, if I found overlooked or lost evidence, I knew that it would be handled correctly. Mostly, I would leave it alone, and place a call on my cell. The forensic teams would arrive quickly because, I'd learned, it was me. My assistants often didn't get the same kind of respect.

Still, asking to see files in a case that had been closed for years was a sensitive thing. It irked all of us involved that we hadn't found the bodies, but, we had consoled ourselves, we had found the killers. I had taken this case as personally as the detectives who had worked it, and we all confessed late one night in the local cop bar that this was the case that haunted us.

Detective Jeffrey Foreno was the only one who had ever expressed doubts about the case. He had openly questioned whether the cult had done the killings. After all, he said, no blood was found in their hidey hole. No knives, no black candles. And nothing suggested they had been on the property that night. It had all been supposition and circumstance, fear and small-town politics.

He had been shushed pretty quickly.

So he was the one I went to that morning.

He was approaching retirement. The lines in his face were deep and grooved, accented by the white stubble he'd forgotten to shave off before coming to work. The rest of his hair was black and thick, in need of a cut. His eyes, once sharp and alert, were blood-shot, and when he saw me, he sighed.

"I knew someone would want to resurrect the dead." He leaned back in his chair, his hands folded over his stomach. "Just didn't expect it to be you."

I'd told him once I dreamed about cleaning the house, about the way the blood came back, as if the walls never wanted to give it up. He'd told me that he dreamed of the case too—of the Christmas tree that hadn't existed even though the outside of the house had been exquisitely decorated, of the lack of food in the kitchen, of the empty pet bowls, cleaned and stored in a dusty pantry.

"Why did you think someone would bring up the case?" I asked, sitting across from him.

He gave me one of those sideways looks that always made me nervous. Even with blood-shot eyes, Jeffrey Foreno had a way of looking all the way to your soul.

"The party," I said.

He pointed at me which, in Jeff language meant *You got it in one.*

"How come you didn't go?" I asked.

"It felt like dancing on someone's grave." Then he gave me that look again and his lips thinned. "You went."

I nodded. "Figured I had to. It had been my job to make sure no one noticed what had happened there."

He didn't move nor did his expression change. "Did it work?"

I shrugged. "I think Louise was using the murders to give the place ambience."

"The power of rubbernecking," he said.

"Yeah." I wouldn't have put it so crassly, but he was right. Maybe that was why I hadn't gone upstairs, why I refused to look at the rooms where the police had assumed most of the killings had taken place. Downstairs, the tree, the presents, the food, masked the prurience that went into the planning. Upstairs, the unvarnished truth—the naked interest on the hands of people more fortunate than the dwellers of the Moorhead House—would have been readily apparent.

"Did it open old wounds?" he asked.

I shook my head quickly, not sure I wanted to examine my answer to that question too closely.

"So you just came today out of curiosity," he said as if he didn't believe it.

"I came because I saw someone." I told him about the waiter, the way the man had looked at me, both at the party and at the courthouse.

Foreno shrugged. "Maybe he was one of the rubberneckers. Some people make certain murder cases into their hobby."

"I know," I said. "But sometimes there's more to it."

He frowned at me.

"Remember anyone involved in the case who looked like that?"

"Like a perfect World War II German? Can't say as I do."

Put that way, I wouldn't have recognized him either. "I'd like to look through the file."

"Be my guest," Fareno said. "It's not going to bother anyone. Unless you find something."

We grinned at each other. Then he led me to records, got me the closed case files, and signed off so that I could work.

***

THE MOORHEAD FILE TOOK UP FIVE BOXES, most of them police and evidence reports. I gave the evidence reports a cursory glance, and saw exactly what I suspected: the assumptions began with the murder of the family and went from there. Most of the blood evidence was scraped from the wall of the bedroom—the crime scene tech's reasoning was simple: he didn't want to deal with the inevitable carpet fibers in the blood pool. Although, to his credit, he did cut carpet swatches as well, and stored them in one of the refrigeration units at the crime lab. Unless someone needed the space, the evidence might still be there.

I searched through the boxes until I found what I was looking for. Pictures. Not of the house, but of the family.

Five members—husband, wife, three children, the oldest being fifteen, the youngest twelve. Speculation by the investigating officer was that one or all of the children had had contact with the cult.

I stared at the father. His face was bony and Aryan too, almost but not quite the same as the waiter I had seen. The eldest son, fourteen, looked like his father or might have if he lived. That heavy bone structure was unusual, at least in these parts. I thumbed through the documents to see if there were other family members in the vicinity.

No one had located any. Pages and pages of police interviews, with neighbors, co-workers, friends, did not include anyone from the family.

Then I looked at the mug shots of the cult members. I remembered those faces from the trial as well. Young, confused, ravaged, they made me wonder whether those kids were vulnerable because they were following the wrong leader or whether they had followed the wrong leader because they were vulnerable.

I closed the boxes, feeling more uncertain than I had before I started. I put them back, and went upstairs to say good-bye to Foreno.

"Find anything?" he asked.

I shook my head.

"Let it rest." Then he gave me that look. "You're not going to, are you?"

"Who inherited the house?" I asked.

"No one," he said. "The state ended up with it."

"No family," I said.

"None that we could find." He tapped a pen against the top of his desk. "And before you ask, let me tell you I remember this because it seemed so damn odd. Two middle-aged parents with no family at all. No one remembered any grandparents or aunts and uncles visiting the kids. These people were an island."

"Their money went to the state too?"

"Eventually," he said. "Not that there was much of it."

"In a house like that?"

"Mortgaged and credit cards. The furniture wasn't even worth anything. The appearance of money, but no real money."

"Don't you find that strange?"

"Always have," he said.

"The guy I saw," I said, "looks a lot like the father."

Foreno cursed, then leaned back in his chair. "You sure?"

"It's not him," I said. "There're differences."

"Family differences?"

"I'd've thought they were brothers or cousins," I said.

Foreno frowned. Then he reached to the left and opened his bottom desk drawer. From my vantage, standing, I could see a dozen accordion files, all filled with manila folders. He thumbed through the files, then pulled out one folder.

He slid it to me, and stood.

"You want some lunch?" he asked. "I'm buying."

I looked at him with surprise.

He nodded toward a chair in the corner. "It'll take you a while to go through that."

"A sandwich would be nice," I said.

He grabbed his suit coat, then headed out the door. As he left, he pulled the door closed, so that someone passing by wouldn't be able to see me.

I found that curious, but not as curious as the file. It was thick with newspaper clippings and computer print-outs, some more than a decade old.

Cult killings, ritual murders, and bodiless cases. This was Foreno's comparison file. He was right: it took me quite a bit of time to read it. He managed to return with the sandwiches and we ate in silence while I read about beheadings and disembowelings, about corpses left in pieces all over property, about candles and black magic and pagan ceremonies.

In each, the bodies remained.

"You don't think they did it," I said, as I tossed my sandwich wrapper into the nearby trash.

"The cult?" He shook his head. "No, I don't think so."

"But the evidence points to them."

"Rather neatly," he said.

"So why didn't you speak up?"

"Because I had no other theory of the case," he said.

"Do you now?" I asked.

"Does your friend work for the catering firm?" And I realized he meant the man with the angular face.

"I think so."

"I'll see if I can track him down."

"And if you do?"

Foreno shrugged. "I'll see what happens next."

***

I WENT BACK TO WORK, thinking about all that blood, all those trails. The carpets were saturated, yet there were no footprints on the hardwood floors, no evidence of someone leaving through the front or back doors. The floors had been well-scrubbed with bleach, and one of the things I testified about was the way that bleach hid all evidence, one of the few things that masked even the goriest scene.

Why, the defense attorney had wanted to know, *would someone remove the footprints, but leave the blood droplets? Why leave the drag marks on the carpet uncleaned?*

I had shrugged. *People aren't that thorough. They clean only what they believe needs cleaning.*

Blood is blood, isn't it? he had asked, implying that someone who cleaned footprints on the hardwood would clean it all.

It's not that simple, I said. *I've had employees who missed spatter on their first few jobs because the scene was too overwhelming.*

Do you think the killer would be overwhelmed? The defense attorney had asked, but the prosecutor had objected to the question. I never got to answer.

Would the killer have been overwhelmed? I considered the question now, at the safety of my desk. Probably not. After all, he created the scene.

Three saturated carpets. Five dead humans. Six quarts of blood per body. That house was soaked, the scene an example—the prosecutor had said—of overkill.

We see what we want to see.

I went back to my notes and, for the first time, did the math.

***

THERE WAS TOO MUCH BLOOD. None of us had realized it. At least twice the amount that should have been in that house. Twice the deaths? Or had someone taken buckets of blood and poured it on the carpets, letting the liquid soak in after he had expertly sprayed the walls.

Reproducing crime scenes wasn't hard. Hollywood did it all the time, and there were photos of other scenes everywhere from forensic journals to true crime novels. Spatter and spray would be easy to reproduce—plant misters, set just right, would mimic the early parts of spray, and something with a bit of kick would be able to reproduce the way that blood spurted from an artery.

There'd be mistakes, but who would look for them? Especially in an overwhelming and fairly obvious scene.

Too much blood wasn't enough for Foreno to reopen the case—it was a closed murder trial, after all. But the blood evidence, coupled with the young man I'd seen, was enough to get Foreno working it again, on the side, in his spare time.

First, he had a crime scene friend re-examine the photos, not explaining anything about the case.

Second, he looked in the Moorhead family background.

Third, he searched for the waiter.

And those three things came together into something both expected and unexpected. The tech said the scene might've been tampered with. Impossible to know now, although the blood was suspicious. Maybe someone else died.

The Moorheads traveled. They were running from debt in Michigan and used charm as well as the co-signature of an old friend to secure the house, which then got them credit cards and a new future.

Until the bank was ready to foreclose. Until the credit card companies had cut them off.

And the co-signer? The same man who had waited tables that night. The one who had overseen the court case. He was living under an alias, one he'd established twenty years before after he had embezzled fifty thousand dollars from a bank in the Midwest.

The bank where his brother had once worked.

The waiter wouldn't talk to the police—hiring a lawyer immediately—but his presence was enough to get those carpet samples tested.

Still refrigerated, still intact after all these years. Sometimes laziness was its own reward.

And that, Foreno said when he came to my office in May, was when it got interesting. The blood was all the same type—O Positive—but that was all it had in common. DNA testing proved that the blood came from dozens of sources, none of them related to the so-called victims.

Just the blood on the wall came from the family and, judging by the overlap in one of the bedrooms, had been applied just like I mentioned, with a sprayer and a lot of determination.

"Why?" I asked. "Why not just disappear? These people were smart enough to create new identities once before."

And that was when he showed me the police files. He'd actually made copies for me so that I could look at them.

Pages and pages and pages of complaints filed by the family, about the neighbors, about the young people in the house at the foot of the hill, about the parties and the goings-on, about the fears of devil worship and a possible cult.

Foreno shook his head. "Looks to me like pure old-fashioned hatred."

"For their neighbors?"

"Their young, unusual, and loud neighbors," Foreno said.

"They set these kids up?" I asked, and felt a shock at myself. I was willing to believe that a cult could off an entire family; I was not willing to believe that a family would set up innocent people in a way that might send them to jail for life.

"Looks like it," he said. "We've got work to do. They've got ten years and a lot of thinking on us."

"But you'll find them," I said.

"I hope so," he said. "But in life, there are no guarantees."

***

EXCEPT ONE.

The story leaked, and the leak coincided with the release of the annual budget. The party, the plans for the museum, and the cost to the taxpayer made page one of our usually sleepy rag.

For a while, it looked like Louise might implode because of the scandal. Then she hit on the right note: the case wouldn't be reopened—innocent people wouldn't be getting out of jail—if she hadn't been interested in the house in the first place.

She had a point, one I didn't care to think about.

Then one afternoon shortly after Halloween, I had to go to the Moorhead House for the final time.

***

I WENT WITH VARIOUS ATTORNEYS—the D.A., several assistants, and defense attorneys for a variety of clients from the waiter to the cult. Someone had found the youngest son in Miami, but he hadn't given up the rest of his family. His very presence—alive—in another state was enough to place doubt on the entire cult-killings story.

He wasn't represented by an attorney, so far as I knew, but I didn't ask a lot of questions.

Instead, I answered them, explaining what chemicals I used, defending myself and why I hadn't noticed the irregularities in the spatter, the extra blood, the lack of footprints.

Over and over again, I said simply that it wasn't my job.

And it wasn't. I was supposed to clean, not think. I was supposed to make the place livable again, and I had.

I had done everything I'd contracted to do.

Maybe that was why the house had haunted me so. Why I had dreamed of it, why the blood kept reappearing on the walls—not as if it couldn't be buried, but as if there was too much of it to contain.

My subconscious had known.

My conscious had refused to accept anything but what it had been told: a family had been murdered by their neighbors, a murderous cult, and the bodies hidden.

Differing interpretations of the same evidence—evidence not examined closely by any of us.

Except the brother, who had made two mistakes. First, he had come to the trial—nervously and obsessively worrying—to see if anyone had found the planted evidence. Or maybe he was stunned and appalled that a case with no bodies generated enough evidence for a conviction. Maybe the family had merely meant to harass the cult, not destroy their lives.

Then he had come back to the house, deliberately getting hired, just so he could see the site of his—and his family's—triumph. Or maybe he had still been worried, still afraid that he would get caught. Maybe he was guarding the place, hoping that no one figured it out.

Or maybe he simply couldn't stay away.

Like I couldn't.

I take evidence of a hideous event and make it vanish. I call that healing, but really, it's just masking. The event remains. It is history; it has happened. I allow people to pretend everything is all right.

What happened in the Moorhead House that day was the opposite of what I do. That family had used a masking technique to get revenge on people they hated, and in the process, managed to disappear with no consequences at all. They left debts, and dozens of families in ruins.

They left a chair pushed out, and knew that we would assume the worst.

We prosecuted based on that assumption, and received a conviction. And I cleaned up the mess so thoroughly that we have to use photographs and cut pieces of rug, miraculously saved. We can't revisit the scene with Luminol, trying to see what had happened before, because I had smeared it, trying to make the home safe, trying to make it—and us—forget.

We'll never know for certain what happened in that house. Just like we'll never know why another neighbor down the street finished his pie last Thanksgiving and then took his own life.

Just like I'll never know how long my mother lay on the floor of her kitchen, conscious and hoping someone would find her.

We can clean the mess, but the uncertainties remain.

There are Christmas lights around the Moorhead House this year, but there will be no party. It's not in the budget. Once the appeals are over, once the trials have ended, the house will become a museum, just like Louise dreamed.

But people aren't going to go inside to look at one of the city's first houses, thinking about old Josiah Moorhead and the power he had because he had the foresight to build ferries that crossed the river. People will go into his house to see if they can find that one piece of evidence, that one spot of blood, that one thing I might have missed in my thorough cleaning, hoping to see if they can solve the case that nearly cost a group of rowdy and unconventional young people their lives.

I won't go back. I'm not going into any damaged houses any more. I'm strictly management now—assigning teams, paying bills. I can't look at interiors filled with the leftovers of other people's lives, and worry that something important has been missed.

I don't want that responsibility.

My imagination is too strong, my memories too fresh.

I don't need any more ghosts.

I have enough already.

Pudgygate

1995

*T*HE WIND OFF THE PACIFIC OCEAN is cold, even in Malibu. A group of fifteen young men huddle close to the celebratory bonfire they have built on a secluded stretch of beach. A short distance away, the cars wait like obedient children. Inside one, a cellular phone rings for the fifth time in an hour.

The sand is still warm from the day's sun. A tapped keg topples like a drunken soldier, but few of the men are drinking any more. They have been talking since noon, catching up on the years since they graduated from Cal Tech and went on their separate ways.

The conversation has deteriorated from highly placed and sometimes top secret research, grant applications, and the possibility of full professorships (as opposed to careers in government science labs) to the kinds of conversations they used to have in the dorm lounges late at night.

Desmond brought up his most embarrassing moment—something to do with toilet paper and the girl's locker room when he was in Middle School—and Benjamin followed with his, Scott with his, and Michael with his.

But the conversation has stopped, for Reuben has taken the stage. Reuben, who took a mysterious trip to London in his senior year, and has refused to talk about it ever since. Reuben is a kind of hero to them all because he crammed two semesters into one that last year, and still managed to graduate with honors.

"Toilet paper on your shoes?" he says as he settles in the center of the circle, legs crossed. He looks like the before picture in a body-building ad, but his skin has cleared in the intervening years, giving him a handsomeness he never possessed before. His hair is longer too, just touching the tips of his tiny ears. "Getting caught peeing on your coach's Volvo? Throwing up all over the Homecoming Queen at the dance? Come on, men, that's kid stuff."

"Kid stuff?" says Scott. His tone is a bit defensive. His Homecoming Queen story did get a lot of laughs.

"Yeah," Reuben says. "Kid stuff. My most embarrassing moment happened at a state dinner when I was in England." And then, because the group does not gasp or do anything else to show that it is impressed, he adds, "In front of Princess Di."

"Princess Di?" asks Benjamin. "*The* Princess Di?"

"Man," says a voice in the blackness. "She's hot. Old, but hot."

"You didn't get sick on her, did you?" asks Scott.

"Not quite," says Reuben, "but it might have been better if I did."

***

WHEN LESTER ASKED ME if I wanted to meet Princess Di (Reuben says, settling into the story-telling cadence he is known for within the group), I never thought it through. I knew Lester had connections—his father was an MP (that's Member of Parliament for you non-anglophiles)—and Lester himself had spent summers with the Royal Family. So I spent my last thousand bucks and skipped the first semester of my final year at Cal Tech to winter in London.

I had brought a tux and my best hair cream. I even thought of getting my nose pierced, but then a friend told me that Di was not an Xer and might find the entire idea a bit gross. (I was a bit relieved; I am prone to sinus infections.)

That same friend sniffed at me for even imagining that anything would come of my meeting with Di. After all, she was a princess and I was a scrawny physics student who knew his way around quarks and computer languages—not the elegant dining rooms of Europe. But I had watched *Pretty Woman* enough to learn about place settings—

("*Pretty Woman*?" Scott says. "You watched *Pretty Woman* more than once?")

("Leave him alone," says Benjamin. "It was a date movie. You did see it on dates, didn't you?")

—and I figured what I didn't know, Lester would teach me.

And teach me he did. Place settings, Waterford crystal, the order of all seven courses. Seems Di had cut back on her social engagements. Lester's family was one of the few receiving her, and while I stayed at the house, I learned not to answer the phone which rang incessantly, particularly in the middle of the night.

This was before the press learned that one of Di's quirks was her penchant for phone harassment. Before the world learned that Di slept with her riding instructor and Charles never loved her. But it was after the bulimia stories, Squidgygate, and the public separation.

Di was lonely.

I hoped to take advantage of that.

Until Lester told me the real reason he had asked me to spend September with his family. They had to host a minor state dinner with the head of state of a small country in the middle of Europe. The Head of State, like the rest of us mortals, was fascinated with Shy Di, and refused to meet with John Major unless he could also meet with Diana. A ticklish thing at best, since at that point, Di was on the farthest outs she could be with the Royals. They refused to socialize with her, and so Lester's father offered, in June, to host the dinner privately.

No one could have known how difficult private had become.

You see, Di was a darling of the international press, and the center of tabloid attention at home. If she wasn't so frail, she probably would have killed a reporter or two by then. The family learned, in July, that hiring a catering staff was out of the question. Half the reporters on Fleet Street now moonlighted for the bigger name restaurants in hopes of a story. So the family had to rely on people they trusted, and when they came up one waiter short, Lester thought of me.

And all those posters of Di in my dorm room.

He figured I was an easy mark. He was right.

(Except for the screaming match the morning I found out. I slammed out of the house, stopped on that quiet English street, with its lovely row of trees, and realized that it was my pride or a chance to gaze on Di in person. I, of course, turned around.)

So, on the night in question, when I should have been wearing my silver tux with my grandfather's diamond cufflinks, I was, instead, wearing a borrowed black tux stained with gravy. The tastefully tight cummerbund covered the gravy stain, but not the feeling of shoddiness it imparted in me. And I still couldn't learn when to serve from the left, and when to serve from the right.

Lester, in exasperation, finally gave up, told me to watch the other waiters—most of whom were as pimply, scrawny and underfed as myself—then retired to his own room to dress for dinner.

Lester would get to eat with the family.

The traitor.

**

THE CHEF WAS REALLY THE GARDENER, a middle-aged Idahonian named (I kid you not) Bubba. Bubba was big, Bubba was strong, and Bubba could protect a princess. But Bubba had only one seven course meal in his rather limited repertoire—a traditional Thanksgiving dinner with all the trimmings. The Americans among the wait staff recognized it and tittered when they realized they were serving a colonial meal to the imperialists. But Bubba took offense at that.

"Them pilgrim guys," he said more than once, "was Brits when they landed on that Rock."

We all agreed, but took a vow of silence anyway. To us, a turkey dinner could never be elegant, not even when it was served on the family's highly polished serving set. And all of us worried, in one way or another, what that infatuated Head of State would think when faced with drumsticks, yams and pumpkin pie.

"Not our problem," said Cletus, the blond All-American hunk who had gone to MIT with Lester during his one summer in Boston. If Di noticed anyone on the wait staff, it would be Cletus.

"Nope. We just gotta make sure we serve this stuff in the best possible way," said Finigan, the tall skinny redhead who had met Lester during that infamous year at the University of Chicago.

"I hope you guys know what goes left and what goes right," I said. I was so nervous my face had broken out in four different places.

"Pay it no never mind," said Bobby Ray, the short, square Louisiana boy who had introduced Lester to Bourbon Street during his brief (and no longer recorded on his transcript) stay at Tulane. "If one of us messes up, all of us mess up. It might be an ice breaker."

"Lester's mother said we weren't to speak to the guests," said Percival, the pasty twenty-five-year old who had yet to reach his adult growth. He had been the class goat, and Lester's bunkmate at Eton during the period Lester called "the hell years."

"Lester's mother," said Georgia, the only girl in the group, with a decided sneer. Georgia was a gum-chewing Angelino of Puerto Rican descent whose black hair was so short, and body was so thin she looked better dressed as a man than all of us except Cletus. "Lester's mother's spine is so straight that she can't bend over to save her life."

Did I say that Georgia predates Lester's Cal Tech period by a wild twenty-four hours that ended in a fight outside the Viper Room? And this time, Lester was not the one caught fighting.

"First course," Bubba said.

We all turned and froze in horror. Dozens of deviled eggs stared up from the shiny silver serving trays like glow-in-the-dark eyeballs.

"These are the appetizers?" Percival asked, his voice small.

"You gotta problem with that?" Bubba crossed his thick arms—his wrists alone were the size of Percival's skull—and frowned.

"Absolutely not," Percival said with more pluck than I had given him credit for. He picked up the first tray, balanced it on his shoulder like a good waiter, and backed out of the swinging door.

As he backed out of the door, Lester's neutered tom, Pudge, sauntered in. Pudge was square as a linebacker, white with a touch of red, and had blue eyes from a roaming Siamese in his family's past. He was also the most focused cat on the planet.

None of us thought much about him, though, since he had never focused on any of us.

Until the salad course.

***

THOSE OF YOU WHO KNOW LESTER should be aware that this was happening in the London Townhouse, not in the 18th century manse in Cheswick or the family estate outside of Kent. For those of you who don't know Lester—well, bear with me a moment while I set the scene.

The brownstone had been remodeled in the recent past by an architect with Vision. The kitchen—which was large enough to seat all of Parliament and still allow someone to cook a meal—was now off the formal dining room. Family dining was down the hall.

"Inconvenience every day of the week except Sunday," Lester liked to say.

Formal dining was a room as large as the kitchen, filled with heavy mahogany furniture, and two chandeliers that looked as if they had once been made for gaslight. A Chinese screen (from some aunt's missionary days) hid the wet bar in the corner. Objets d'art lined the shelves on the walls—collectible plates (which Lester assured me *were not* limited editions from the Franklin Mint), antique vases (pronounced vaaaaazes), and chipped, ugly statues from some uncle's Egyptian salad days. (At the other formal meal I attended, the guy from the British Museum drooled over those damaged things and claimed that the family might want to do a public service and donate the statues, particularly the one of Horus which even I knew was worth something because it had rubies instead of eyes. Nothing more was said. Public service, apparently, is not Lester's family's forte.)

The guests mingled in the library which Lester's parents had settled on after a heated debate ("The front parlor has your family's hideous weapons collection," snapped Lester's mother, "which is not something a young woman in the middle of a marital crisis should see, or have access to, for that matter!") and sipped expensive liquor while Bubba finished the first course.

We were to put the appetizers on the table, and then the butler would call the family into dinner. We tried to arrange the serving platters of eggs as far away from the lights as possible, but the butler (who had been with the family nearly fifty years) still blanched. Nonetheless, he went off to perform his duty, and we fled the room.

In the kitchen, Pudge sat in front of the hot stove, staring at the roasting turkey inside. Bubba was preparing the second course—the soup course—for which (it soon became apparent) he had special-ordered a case of Campbell's Chicken Noodle from the States. The sound of the can opener didn't arouse Pudge who was more intent on the sizzling bird than even the opportunity for cat food.

We had ten minutes to debate the best serving method for soup while Bubba zapped individual bowls in the microwave. ("Are you supposed to do that with fine china?" Georgia asked. "You seen anything else I should use?" Bubba countered.) He topped each boiling bowlful with a sprig of parsley then sent us on our way.

The soup course allowed us to get our first glimpse of the guests.

The foreign Head of State (whom we were to refer to as Your Honored and Respected Sir, if we were to refer at all) wore a dark gray tux that accented his silvering hair. His face, unlined thanks to some obvious plastic surgery, had all the warmth of the Tower of London. His wife, wearing a gown covered with tiny diamonds, looked like an aging Barbie doll. Lester's family filled the gaps in the table. And Di, even though she was surrounded by a crowd of people, sat alone.

She wore a tiny tiara in her hair that matched the choker around her neck. Her dress was off the shoulder, revealing the slight rise of her breasts. She smiled as she flirted with the Head of State, but the smile never reached her eyes. Her voice had an airy, little girlish tone that I hadn't noticed in her public speeches. She ate part of an egg, leaving a dainty half-moon on her plate.

I whisked the plate away. Wonder of wonders, miracle of miracles, I had been assigned to Di's chair. Lester winked at me as I whisked with one hand, and set with the other.

Di's hair smelled of jasmine, and I bent so close to her I could feel the warmth of her skin.

I managed to place the soup bowl without spilling a drop.

Di didn't even notice.

And then, all too soon, it was over. We carried the dirty dishes back to the kitchen (to be dealt with by the morning's cleaning crew), and to await our next task.

Cletus went to the window to count the bodyguards the Princess had brought with her. Finigan went to the other window to see if he could tell the Princess's guards from the foreign head's of state. Georgia kibitzed from the back, betting they couldn't tell the Lester's family guards from the guest's guards.

I sat on a chair near the stove, which put me right next to Pudge. He was still staring at the turkey, his big blue eyes shining with fascination.

He had been at the stare-down over an hour now, and showed no signs of moving.

Bubba, on the other hand, was circling the kitchen like a man possessed. He was finally in his element. The salad course featured greens from his garden, topped with all sorts of veggies Great and Small. The veggies were nurtured by Bubba's large, but capable hands, and he treated them like precious children as he put the finishing touches on the plates.

For once, a dish I would be proud to serve to a Princess. The salad looked like something out of a restaurant, with onions sliced so thin they looked like tiny bracelets resting on top of the romaine.

The dressing boats were on the table (I had already checked when I saw Bubba and learned there was going to be a salad course), so we had nothing to worry about.

"Hey, Bubs," Georgia said. "What comes next after the salad?"

Bubba set the last plate on a tray and then grabbed potholders. "Not sure," he said. "Been thinking maybe the cranberries can be a course all by themselves."

"You're not certain?" Percival asked, his face going whiter than the butler's had when he saw the eggs. "Good God, man, this is a state dinner!"

"What do you care?" Gently, with a booted foot, Bubba shoved Pudge aside, and opened the oven door. The rich smell of roast turkey filled the kitchen. Pudge stood and approached the open door.

"Why, sir," Percival said, "I care because we, the wait staff, will have to suffer the displeasure of the guests should the meal not be, how should I say it, up to snuff."

"He means if they don't like it, we get all the flak," Bobby Ray said.

"I know what he means." Bubba pushed Pudge aside again. Then Bubba bent at the waist and hauled the turkey out of the oven. The bird was huge, golden brown, and the juices dripped from its sides into the pan below. Bubba might not know how to cook soup, but he sure knew his turkey.

He put the turkey on the counter near the sink, then grabbed the pots filled with potatoes, and placed them on the stovetop. Then he opened the refrigerator and pulled out six pies. The fillings were loose, but I recognized them anyway: pumpkin, mincemeat, and apple. He put those in the now-empty oven.

"You can bake them all at the same temperature?" I asked.

"What is everybody, a critic?" Bubba snapped. "You try cooking a meal for the Princess a Wales. At least you guys geta look at her."

Georgia left her spot at the window and came into the kitchen. She took a piece of romaine off the nearest salad.

"Now, now, Bubba," she said, sounding not at all reassuring. "We simply want this meal to go as well as you do."

"I been working on this for the last week and—dang!" Bubba slapped a meaty hand against his own forehead. "Babe, can you open the cranberries? And kid—" he was looking at me "—I need you ta take the bread outta that fancy warming pan thing."

It took me a moment to locate the fancy warming pan thing, which proved a nice distraction so that neither Bubba or Georgia saw me grin while she harangued him for calling her Babe. I took the bread out, and ar-ranged the slices in the wicker baskets that Bubba had left near the warming pan thing (which looked, in case you're wondering, like a giant metal bread box with a heater).

By the time I turned around, Georgia was opening large cans of imported cranberry jelly (the flat kind that takes the form of the can), Bubba was putting shredded Parmesan on the salad, and Pudge on the counter beside the turkey, happily nibbling the knobby end of a drumstick.

"Pudge!" I screamed from across the room. Bubba whirled, but Percival beat him to the cat's side. Pudge got tossed halfway across the kitchen, and slid on the tiled floor before he could skid to a stop near the back door. Cletus opened the door and tried to toss Pudge out, but a burly guard blocked the way.

"So sorry," the guard said. "No one leaves."

"Not me," Cletus said. "The cat."

"Right-o," the guard said, shrugging a bit. "Fraid I do have my orders. You never know what that cat could be concealing on his person."

"Half the princess's turkey," Finigan said.

"What?" the guard said.

"Nothing." Cletus slammed the door closed. Pudge hung from his arms, square body extended, all limbs pointing toward the turkey. His little jaw was still work-ing its last bite and his pale blue eyes were still focused on the bird, now all the way across the room.

"Great," Finigan said. "Now what do we do with him?"

"We must serve the salad," Percival said. "It's past time."

"Yeah," Georgia muttered. "We don't want to leave them alone with that soup too long."

Bubba glared at her, but she pretended not to notice. Bobby Ray peered at the gnawed drumstick. "He only took the skin off the edge. If we peel all the skin away from that part of the bone no one will notice."

"Get out of here. You're distracting me," Bubba said.

"What about Pudge?" Cletus asked.

"Cat won't get past me a second time." Bubba literally snarled the words. He spoke with such force, I actually looked around to see if there was a cleaver handy, and sighed with relief when there wasn't.

"Okay," Cletus said. He put Pudge down. The cat zoomed like a smart missile for the turkey.

"You're covered with hair!" Georgia said, and it was true. White cat hair coated the front of Cletus's tux.

"We're exceedingly late," Percival said. "The butler just gave us A Look through the door."

"No one'll notice the hair in the dim lighting," Finigan said. "Let's go."

We grabbed our salad trays and hurried into the dining room. The soup bowls were empty. As I whisked Di's away, and replaced it with her salad plate (another lovely, deft, almost professional maneuver which she didn't notice), I overheard the Head of State's wife ask if she could get the chef's soup recipe.

Georgia snorted and Lester glared at her. "Sorry, ma'am," said Bobby Ray, who was responsible for the wife's eating enjoyment. "Closely guarded family secret."

And we all managed to stumble into the kitchen before collapsing with the giggles.

**

In the kitchen, Bubba was making gravy. Sweat beaded on his forehead and he bit his lower lip with the concentration of a man taking the SAT test. He was swaying back and forth as if stirring made him dizzy.

The turkey cooled on the counter, Pudge-less.

It wasn't until I got all the way inside the room that I understood.

Bubba was standing on one booted foot. With the other, he was blocking Pudge who was trying to get into proper position to jump onto the counter. Much of the floor was spattered with gravy, and Pudge's whiskers had some suspicious smudges.

"Someone get that cat," Bubba said. "He don't even want no gravy. Not while that turkey's in the room."

"Give him the heart," Georgia said. "That should keep him busy for a while."

"Good idea," Cletus said.

"You do it," Bubba said. "If I stop now, we're gonna get lumps."

Cletus pulled the heart, neck, and liver from their places on the turkey's side. Each movement he made left little white cat hairs all over the counter.

"Yuck," Finigan said. "Did you do that to Lester's mother's salad?"

"Sure hope so," Cletus said with a grin.

Percival had taken over blocking duties from Bubba. For each move that Percival made, Pudge made a new one, never taking his steely-eyed gaze from the turkey. From my perspective, it looked as if Pudge and Percival were involved in a ritual dance.

Finally Cletus finished carving Pudge's meal. He waved the plate under the cat's nose—

("Hey!" Bubba shouted. "That was one of my dessert plates!")

—and then carried the plate to the back door. Pudge followed, tail high, looking as proud as if he had bagged the bird himself.

"I've been thinking," Georgia said, "that we should serve the turkey and fixings as one course, and dessert as the final course."

"That's only five," Bubba said, still stirring. "I was supposed ta do seven."

"I don't think anyone will miss the other two," Georgia said.

"What were you planning to serve after the, ah, cranberry course?" Percival asked.

"The bread course, what else?" Bubba wiped his forehead with the back of his left hand, revealing a sweat stain the size of California in his armpit.

"What else?" Georgia mouthed behind his back.

"Sounds good," Cletus said as he walked away from Pudge. The cat was gobbling his food so fast we could hear the sucking sounds across the room. "But I wanna go home sometime tonight. How about we just do what Georgia said. I'm sure they're not gonna mind either. I mean, how long would you want to spend with Lester's mom?"

"Good point," Bubba said. He pulled the gravy off the burner. "Don't make no difference to me. If anyone asks, I'll just say you guys dropped the other two courses."

"Should we break some plates as a cover?" Bobby Ray asked.

"Lord, no!" Percival said. "Do you know how much these dishes are worth?"

"It was a joke, Percy," I said, unable to take the strain any longer. In two contacts, Di hadn't even looked at me. I didn't know how to get her attention without making a fool of myself. And I was getting tired of standing in this kitchen.

"Okay," Bubba said. "You guys go clear the salad and put out dinner plates. By the time you get back, I'll have everything in their proper serving stuff."

We did as we were told. Out in the formal dining room, the conversation had turned to future of the monarchy, and Lester's father was desperately trying to turn it to something else. Di looked as if she were going to cry at any moment.

She hadn't touched her salad.

I whisked the plate away and replaced it with a larger piece of the family china.

"What is this?" Lester's mother whispered loudly to Cletus. "The invisible course?"

The butler, who was pretending to supervise, placed his hands behind his back and walked toward the table.

Percival glanced in the butler's direction, and stammered, "Ah, we-we-we are br-br-bringing the main course now, ma'am."

I didn't have long to ponder what childhood memories the butler's approach raised in Percival because Di put her cool fingers on my arm. I glanced down at her manicured hand, resting so softly on my naked wrist, and I thought I had died and gone to heaven.

"Would you be so kind as to bring me a spot of tea? I do know it's out of order, but I would be ever so grateful."

Ah, gratitude. A man always likes that in a woman. It might lead her to…express it. "Certainly, your Highness," I said, and cringed as I mimicked her accent.

("Is that the embarrassing moment?" Scott asks, his sneer ready.

("No," Reuben says crossly.

("Good," Scott says. "Because if it is, make up something better, okay?")

She didn't even notice. She returned to the discussion of the monarchy by saying that she was concerned for William and Harry's future. I didn't get to hear the rest of the thought as we carried the dirty dishes into the kitchen. A huge stack of expensive but filthy china stood on the counter above the family's American-style dishwasher.

"Ain't none of them ate their salad?" Bubba asked with obvious disappointment.

"Too pretty to touch," I said, taking pity.

No one could say that about the rest of the meal. The turkey was piled haphazardly on the platters ("Didn't anyone ever show you the old one platter for white, one platter for dark routine?" Georgia asked). The potatoes looked like the snow cap on Mount Shasta. The cranberries were standing in perfect, wiggly can-shaped circles on their plates ("My mom used to at least slice it," Finigan said as he picked up the cranberry dishes and put them on the tray). And the yams looked like wizened overcooked tubers in the center of perfectly white bowls (but then they always looked like that to me). There were no garden veggies because Bubba had used them all for the salads.

And to make matters worse, no one had remembered to put on water for tea.

Bubba promised to do so while we delivered the food. I hoped he would remember. He had to deal with the turkey carcass first. Pudge was done with his little dinner and it obviously had not been enough.

"Land Shark," Cletus said, looking at the white cat circling Bubba's legs.

"Food's getting cold," Bubba said.

"The tea's for the Princess," I said again, just in case he forgot.

"Ain't it always?" Bubba muttered.

I got the turkey platters on my large server's tray and led the charge into the dining room. "Your tea is coming, Your Highness," I said as I set a platter next to Di.

She smiled at me and I felt the look all the way to my toes. I didn't even notice when the lights went out, thinking in my dazed state that the world had simply gone dark with the force of my joy.

Lester's mother screamed. His father shouted something about getting the torch (I sure hoped that was a flashlight), and the Head of State whistled for his personal body guard. Behind me came the sound of breaking glass. Bubba was yelling in the kitchen, and the swinging door slammed into the wall. I felt a rush of wind as something flew past me. I set the platter down quickly so I wouldn't drop it on Di. She had made not a sound.

"Get it off me! Get it off, I say!" quavered a querulous male voice that I didn't recognize.

The thin beam of a flashlight revealed a mess at the table. The Head of State and his wife were quivering at the far wall. Di was sitting rigidly. Lester was running out of the room—for the bodyguards I hoped—and the wait staff was frozen in mid-service.

The butler was screaming and groping with his right hand at a furry white thing braced on his shoulder. Pudge whipped his little head around. He had overshot his target, but now, with the aid of the light, he saw his quarry.

The turkey platters.

He launched himself at the table.

Lester's father brought his hand up to protect his face, lost his grip on the light, and it crashed to floor, placing us in darkness again.

Part of my brain registered the oddness of the butler's movements. Why fight a determined cat with one hand? Then the breaking glass registered.

"The butler did it!" I shouted, and ran for him. Amazingly, I reached him, grabbed him, and held him long enough for Lester's father to recover the light.

The circle of light waved around the room. In the front of the house, the bodyguards pounded on the door. Bubba was still shouting in the kitchen, accompanied by more breaking glass. The butler was struggling, and I could barely hold him. Cletus and Bobby Ray hurried to my side as the beam of light caught the butler's left hand.

He was holding the statue of Horus, the one with the ruby eyes.

"Cedric!" said Lester's father. "Whatever are you doing?"

"It fell, sir," the butler said.

Cletus and Bobby Ray grabbed the butler's arms.

"Yeah," I said. "It fell after he broke the glass."

"Good heavens," said Lester's mother as the flashlight beam wavered and went out.

"Lester!" said his father. "Didn't you replace the batteries?"

They argued for a few minutes, the front and back doors crashed in simultaneously, and then the chandeliers came back on. "The pies!" Bubba wailed.

The Head of State and his wife were still cowering in the corner. Lester was standing beside the butler, holding the man's collar like a bounty hunter, Cletus and Bobby Ray holding him for real. The rest of the wait staff still retained their various positions.

"Pudge!" Lester's mother said, her tone revealing her shock at this newest horror.

We all looked at the cat. He was standing in the potatoes, and leaning over the turkey platter. A piece of white meat dangled from his dainty, overworked mouth.

Tears rolled down Diana's face, and she was shaking. I wanted to put a hand on her shoulder to comfort her, but couldn't.

"Your Highness, are you all right?" Lester's father asked.

Diana nodded, then burst into a gale of laughter. "I haven't had this much fun," she managed between chuckles, "since I quit teaching kindergarten."

***

THE FIRE IS BURNING LOW. The ocean rumbles behind them. Benjamin throws the last log onto the pyre.

"I don't get it," Michael says. "The butler did what?"

"He was trying to steal the Egyptian art," Scott says.

"But why?" Michael says. "He had plenty of time to do that during the day."

Reuben shakes his head. "That's what we all thought, but it actually makes a curious kind of sense. You see, any theft would be traced back to him. But he figured on that night any disturbance would be credited to the press following Princess Di. He had drugged the coffee for the guards in the sitting room and library, and had already lifted some small items from those rooms. He also did some damage to the furniture to make it look like the losses were breakage. By the time the thefts were discovered, he planned to have sold the pieces to some black marketeers, and to be long gone."

"I thought you said only trusted servants were on that night," someone says from the darkness in the back.

"Well," Reuben says, "he had been with the family for decades. How much more trusted can you get?"

"What, did he just snap?" Scott asks.

"Naw," Reuben says. "I think he saw it as his last chance to get rich before he died."

Wood crackles in the bonfire. A big wave crashes against the shore. Small white clouds look like cotton against the blackness of the sky.

"I still don't get it," Scott says. "I mean, mimicking Di's accent is nowhere near as embarrassing as losing your lunch on the Homecoming Queen."

"That wasn't the embarrassing moment," Reuben says, looking down at his hands.

"That's the only one that comes close as far as I can tell," Scott says.

"Yeah, right now you kinda sound like a hero," Michael adds.

"Well, actually," Reuben says, "I left out the embarrassing part. When the flashlight went out the second time, I kissed Di."

"So what's wrong with that? I woulda done it," Benjamin says.

"Me, too."

"And me."

The rest of the group choruses their agreement. Reuben has not looked up from his hands. He clenches them into fists.

"And she said, in a very calm, mannered voice, 'Lester, I do believe one of your friends has just committed a crime against the state.'"

Someone chokes back a laugh.

"Shows she's got a sense of humor," Benjamin says at last.

"A vicious one," Reuben says. He turns his head away from the bonfire so that the group can't see his expression. "'You should tell him,' she continued, 'that the next time he plans to kiss a Princess, he should brush his teeth first.'"

"Jeez," someone says.

"And then she started laughing, only she wasn't making a sound, so I thought she was crying."

The group is silent, all imagining themselves at the side of the Princess of Wales who, although she is old, is hot. Then they all imagine she is so grossed out by their kiss that she says something about it. They shudder in unison.

Finally Scott, who feels responsible for prying this story out of Reuben says, "Hey, man, I bet no one knew it was you. All the waiters were Lester's friends."

Reuben shakes his head. "At that very moment, the lights came up. The only waiter who was blushing was me."

Silence again. Unlike the homecoming story which has, for these men, a slight undertone of an ice goddess getting her just desserts, Reuben's story carries its own level of pity. After all, the embarrassment is on an international scale.

"Then what?" Michael asks softly.

"What do you mean 'then what'?" Reuben says.

"What did you do then?"

Reuben licks his lips and glances at a faraway place none of them can see. "She took my hand and, wiping the tears from her eyes, said, 'If you are a love and bring me my tea, I'll give you a right proper kiss.'"

"And did you get her tea?" Scott asks.

For the first time since dark, Reuben grins. "After I brushed my teeth," he says.

He looks at the cars parked in a line against the side of the road. Almost as if on cue, a cellular phone inside one car rings for the sixth time in the last hour.

"Aren't you ever going to answer that?" Scott asks.

Reuben shakes his head. "She'll call back," he says. "She always does."

Scrawny Pete

*H*E FOUND SCRAWNY PETE, flea-bitten, hair coming out in patches, and eyes like a baby's, in a fifth floor walk-up, crouched beside two dead bodies. The cat wouldn't come to anyone but him, and in a moment of weakness, he took the damn thing. The vet'd cleaned him up, put antibiotics on the scabs, gave Atkins some salve and some special food and sent him on his way.

A cat owner.

And not just any cat. Scrawny Pete was on his way to becoming a legend.

The dead bodies had been part of a domestic. Typical, in its way. Murder-suicide. Always seemed that the man shot the woman and ate the gun. Fifteen years on the crime beat for whichever daily tabloid paid him enough to write his five hundred words of wisdom showed him that there was nothing in the human existence that someone didn't try to solve with a gun. In the mouth, out of the mouth, in the heart, in the stomach, it didn't matter. In America, someone whipped out a gun and entire lives ended. A flash, an instant, leaving more heartbreak than any newspaper could cover.

As if it wanted to. Whoever said, "All happy families are alike, but all unhappy families are unhappy in their own ways," had been more right than Atkins wanted to imagine.

The problem with Scrawny Pete, as Atkins soon learned, was that the damn cat was terrified of being alone. Surprisingly, loud noises didn't bother him, and neither did the smell of blood, but his own company in the quiet of Atkins's apartment drove the cat absolutely crazy. Atkins tried leaving the television on, and bringing home a kitten, but Scrawny Pete was intelligent enough to know that a TV wasn't company, and he didn't tolerate any furry companions in his fancy abode.

Somehow the damn cat talked Atkins into taking him everywhere. Atkins started wearing a great coat with a large pocket that Scrawny Pete—who was smaller than most six-month-old kittens—took to riding in. Atkins found that Pete could be smuggled anywhere, restaurants, hotels, even doctor's offices. And once he started writing about Pete in his column, well, he didn't have to smuggle the cat anywhere any more.

It was June 21st, one year to the day after he'd gotten Scrawny Pete, that he found himself taking an old Otis to the top floor of a scrungy apartment building on the lower East Side. The cops were already on the scene. Some rookie was standing outside the main door, arms crossed, unwilling to let in any comers even with press badges until he saw Scrawny Pete. Atkins mumbled as the Otis's doors slid open on the fourteenth floor that if he'd known a cat was worth more than a press badge he'd've gotten the cat years ago.

Scrawny Pete had no answer. If anything, the cat seemed tenser than usual.

Pete was always unnaturally tense. Atkins attributed it to the poor critter's upbringing by such obviously happy folk. He could only imagine how awful it had been. The walk-up hadn't had any cat food. The only sign that a cat had even lived there were the claw marks on the living room sofa. Obviously the happy couple had let Scrawny Pete fend for his dinner in the hall with the other stray cats, and had let him live the bulk of his life outside—which had probably been good for Scrawny Pete or he might have been the first to taste the gun, long before hubby decided the family needed a vacation in Never-Never-Land.

But in this hallway, which smelled of grease and garlic and Asian cooking, overlaid with filth and a bit of despair, Pete's naturally tense body became a hard little wire. Atkins put a hand on Pete's back, like he used to do when they first started traveling together, before he realized that nothing—not honking horns, not screaming people, not the breeze from a passing train—could spook Pete enough to make him leave the pocket. Pete's security was Atkins, and that cat wasn't ever going to let go.

Apartment 14A had a crooked metal sign and an open presswood door, the outside of which had once seen the backside of someone's foot. The breaks in the wood weren't new and they weren't clean, and all they left was a thin layer of really cheap oak covering between the inhabitants—or former inhabitants as the case might be—and the rest of the world.

Atkins pushed his way inside, felt Pete turn into a statue against his side and start making little huffing noises. Two detectives stood inside, both in plainclothes, cheap off-the-rack suits that had seen better days. The ME stood over the bodies with the department's camera, preserving the scene for posterity, although it was obvious what had happened.

Husband shot the wife before eating the gun. The air still had an acrid whiff from the double discharge. Atkins was surprised he could smell it over the stench of blood and voided bowels.

The detectives recognized him, showed him where to stand so that he wouldn't violate the scene. Pete was still huffing, his fur rising on his back. Strange behavior. Stranger way still to spend their one-year anniversary.

Atkins stared at the couple. Young, by the looks of their hands. Poor, by the looks of the apartment. But not that poor, by the looks of their stuff. In fact, a bit upscale for a neighborhood like this.

"Slumming, Atkins?" one of the detectives asked.

"Heard the call," he said, hand still on Pete. "What is it about this day, hm? It's not Christmas. Not nothing at all. What makes people go off on this day?"

"What?" the detective said. "There been other calls today?"

Atkins shook his head. "A year ago today, I got Pete at a place just like this one. In fact…" His voice trailed off. He shuddered, something he hadn't done at a crime scene in more than a decade.

"What?" the detective asked, but Atkins ignored him. Instead he crouched, put his hands up to his face as if he were forming a camera, and looked through the frame.

"Do bodies always fall like that in a murder-suicide?" he asked.

"Like what?" the detective asked.

"Side by side, twinned up like they're in bed next to each other, only they're on the floor."

"Naw." The answer came from the ME. He'd taken the last shot. "Usually, they are in bed. It's only a few who do it in the middle of the living room. I think they had some kind of argument, he grabs the gun, waves it in her face, she thinks he ain't gonna do nothing, maybe even dares him, he shoots, realizes what he's done, then shoots himself."

Sounded plausible.

Pete was making little sounds of distress. Atkins put his hand back in his pocket. Pete was shivering. In the whole past year, in all the strange situations, he'd never once felt Pete shiver. Not even in the middle of winter.

"Never figured you for one of them animal lovers who took his friggin pet everywhere," the other detective said.

Atkins shrugged, pretended an indifference he didn't really feel. "It gets readers."

"Sure does," the first detective said. "The wife reads your column now like you're writing the adventures of Scrawny Pete. You should mention him every day."

"Yeah," Atkins said. "He sure has a place in a story like this one."

"I don't see no story here," the ME said. "Sad to tell, but who really cares when some guy takes out himself and his wife. 'Cept the friends and family, of course."

Atkins looked at him. The ME was a skinny redhead with premature aging lines from frowning instead of too much sunlight. "No kids?" he asked.

"Not a one."

"How common is that?"

The ME shrugged. "I'm not a walking book of statistics."

"I mean, isn't it usually long-marrieds, or newly separateds, or bad divorces who resort to this?"

"Can't say." The ME looked over his shoulder. But one of the detectives frowned.

"Where you going with this, Atkins?"

"Nowhere," he said. "Just seems strange to me. The couple that I got Pete from, they were in this position, no kids, dead in the living room in a fifth floor walk-up not a lotta different from this."

"The world's weird, Atkins," one of the detectives said. "Who'd've figured? It's like you and that crazy cat."

"Yeah," Atkins said softly, not taking his hand off Pete. "Who'd've figured."

***

It DIDN'T STOP HIM from checking anyway. Superstition was sometimes a reporter's best friend. He and Pete spent the afternoon digging through records, and what he found chilled him. The past five years, there'd been a murder-suicide on the same date. Same day, same pose, different precincts. No one recognized the scene. And because it was looked like a murder-suicide, no one did more than a cursory investigation. Did he shoot her? Yeah. Did he shoot himself? Yeah. End of story.

But not really.

Atkins called the detective in charge of the latest one, told him what he'd learned, and didn't explain how he got his hunch, except to say that he remembered the anniversary of getting Pete.

Pete was still freaked. Atkins had learned, in the year he'd had Pete, that cats had memories, emotional memories, like people. The apartment drove him crazy; whenever one of the neighbors got to shouting, Pete dove under the couch. He sat in the corner like a terrified rabbit when Atkins wasn't home, not moving at all, defecating and urinating in the spot where Atkins left him in the morning. He'd done that for a week before Atkins, who knew that Pete understood a litter box, tried taking Pete to work.

The rest, of course, was history.

The detective didn't call back for two days. By then, Atkins was three columns away from the scene.

He remembered it, of course. That night, Pete had slept like a baby in his arms, something he wouldn't admit to anyone, barely admitted to himself, and the cat seemed spookier than usual. But life marched on and Atkins with it, turning in his five hundred words, crime beat, the most popular column in the city with or without mention of Scrawny Pete.

"Atkins," the detective said.

"Yeah?"

"You got a story here. Want it? We wouldn'ta got it without you."

Reporters lived for calls like that. Atkins was no different, even after fifteen years. He went to the precinct, which was gray and dirty and smelled like ancient coffee, just like every other precinct in the city, and listened as the detective explained, in excruciating detail, how they went over the crime scene, how they found things that didn't exactly fit: a shoe mark in blood that didn't belong to any of the cops; a handprint on the coffee table; fibers in the wounds that had nothing to do with either deceased.

The detective didn't apologize. He knew that Atkins was a pro, Atkins understood how overworked they all were, how they liked to close cases, especially easy ones, like a murder-suicide, how hard sometimes serial killings were to see.

Luckily, or so the detective said, this one was easily solved. A neighbor—one Tobias Craig—heard the fighting, complained, complained again, finally decided to take matters into his own hands. Apparently he snapped every June 21st. Left a visible trail once they knew what to look for. Every apartment super with the June 21 murders remembered the guy complaining about the noise.

The cops had interviewed him at every scene and he'd always been the one who said the expected litany: *It don't surprise me, officers. They were fighting all the time.*

Atkins knew better than to ask for a why, but he got it anyway: Apparently Craig's name was all over the system, not as a criminal, but as a victim. Parents dead of a murder-suicide—a confirmed one—that happened in front of the children on June 21st, 1979. He'd been six at the time.

Atkins found the clippings, saw the blood-spattered children being led out of the apartment. In his imagination watched them watching their father pull out the gun like the ME had said, pull the trigger, kill his wife, then in sudden remorse, kill himself. He'd forgotten the children, sleeping in the next room, the children who'd crawled out of their shared bed to see what the noise was just in time to watch him eat his gun.

Scrawny Pete'd seen it of course. That explained the terrors, the fears of being left alone with neighbors who shouted and screamed. Was he their cat, the dead couple's? Or had he originally been a stray who'd taken food from Craig? No telling, and certainly Pete wouldn't say. Not in any way Atkins wanted to see anyway.

So he wrote the column, asked if it could go on more than 500 measly words, and because he rarely asked, and because his longer columns usually got national attention, sometimes awards, his editor said sure. Atkins wrote the story, mentioning Pete's reaction to the smells, the repeated scene. Mentioning, only mentioning. And then he'd gone on to reflect on the way the system failed the victims and the way it created more victims and was it guns or the human race's innate violence that caused a man to shoot his wife and then himself, to start a ball rolling that would leave five couples dead after some kind of terror at the hands of a crazy man who'd once been a blood-spattered six-year-old kid.

People didn't remember the analysis or the arguments or the excellent prose, some of the best of his career. Nope. They remembered the bizarre nature of the story, and they remembered Pete. And over the years, it became the crime that Pete solved, and Scrawny Pete became a legend.

Atkins didn't mind. Cats could become legends. Reporters shouldn't. Reporters schlepped from scene to scene, observing, recording, trying to make sense out of one corner of the world. Sometimes he managed it, sometimes he didn't. But he was the best at it, for a few years at least.

The years he had Scrawny Pete in his pocket.

Stomping Mad: A Spade Conundrum

S HE CALLED HERSELF the Martha Stewart of Science Fiction, and she looked the part: Homecoming-queen pretty with a touch of maliciousness behind the eyes, a fakely tolerant acceptance of everyone fannish, and an ability to throw the best room party at any given Worldcon in any given year.

So when a body was found in her party suite, the case came to me. Folks in fandom call me the Sam Spade of Science Fiction, but I'm actually more like the Nero Wolfe: a man who prefers good food and good conversation, a man who is huge, both in his appetite and in his education. I don't go out much, except to science fiction conventions (a world in and of themselves) and to dinner with the rare comrade. I surround myself with books, computers, and televisions. I do not have orchids or an Archie Goodwin, but I do possess a sharp eye for detail and a critical understanding of the dark side of human nature.

I have, in the past, solved over a dozen cases, ranging from finding the source of a doomsday virus that threatened to shut down the world's largest fan database to discovering who had stolen the Best Artist Hugo two hours before the award ceremony. My reputation had grown during the last British Fantasy Convention when I—an American—worked with Scotland Yard to recover a diamond worth £1,000,000 that a Big Name Fan had forgotten to put in the hotel's safe.

But I had never faced a more convoluted criminal mind until that Friday afternoon at the First Annual Jurassic Parkathon, a media convention held in Anaheim.

***

THE CONVENTION was officially called Dinocon I because Crichton's people, or Spielberg's people, or some studio's people wouldn't give permission to use the Jurassic Park name with a non-sanctioned project. I normally don't get involved with a media con, especially one held in Anaheim, but this one had a million dollar budget and a state-of-the-art computer system, and I simply couldn't resist the challenge.

So I was in Ops with most of the folks running the con when the call came through. Ops, for those of you who've never seen one, is a hotel function room with most of the furniture removed, replaced with tables covered with computer equipment, too many chairs, and tons of print out paper. Most of the people working Ops look haggard and stressed by the time the convention starts, and many of them are ready to collapse by the time it's over. So we really didn't need to hear some security person, young by the sound of him, on the two-way radio:

"Hey, ah, we got a, um, Situation X, here."

Everyone in Ops snapped to attention. The actual term was a File X—always a pun, everything a pun—and it was only supposed to be used for an extreme emergency.

"Copy that," Doris, a muscular woman the size of Stallone, said. She headed security, and had at every major con I'd ever worked on. Security is important at sf conventions, perhaps *the* most important thing, because these cons, as most of you know, aren't your simple suit-tie-and-briefcase affairs. The big conventions have three levels: the fans, most of whom dress in costume (some medieval barbarians, some Captain Kirk, some space aliens); the pros, most of whom write, act, or somehow work in the science fiction field; the dealers, most of whom sell sf paraphernalia—books, videos, posters, and the ubiquitous Bajoran earrings. Media cons had more earrings, videos, and actors; fewer books, writers, and intellectual discussions. Behind it all is the con-com, the army of people who run the entire shebang, and put out any and all fires along the way. Security deals with most of those: from regular hotel guests who are scared by the werewolf in the elevator to the teenagers who've stayed up all night playing the card game *Magic*, and who suddenly think it fun to pull the fire alarm on the second floor.

Never, in my twenty years of fandom, have we gotten a call for this kind emergency, and never have I heard a security person sound so scared.

"It's in room 4708. Can someone come here?" The security kid's voice cracked, confirming my suspicion: he was a volunteer, and he was eighteen at most.

"What's the nature of the emergency?" Doris asked.

"I don't think you want me to describe it on an open channel," the kid said.

"All right, be right there," Doris said, and left.

We mused about the "Situation" X for a moment. "Maybe," Ruth, the con chair, said, "he saw a fur bikini for the first time."

"It's the masquerade tonight," John said behind her, and we all laughed. He probably saw a costume, got scared, and decided to call it in. We'd all had that happen before.

"Or maybe it's pea soup," said Ben, and I, being most senior on the staff, groaned. I remembered that one, which had now eased into fannish legend. Just after *The Exorcist* came out, some fans in Baltimore held a room party and served pea soup along with the usual potato chips, cheese, and beer. After midnight, when the crowd got really drunk, someone had the brilliant idea of imitating Linda Blair in the famous vomit sequence. Of course, everyone had to do it, and by the time security arrived, a sea of pea soup was running down the corridor like the Blob without the assistance of the special effects people.

"Please, ghod, anything but that," I said.

At that moment, the phone rang. Ruth answered, and handed it to me, her tired face filled with confusion and surprise. "It's Doris," she said. "For you."

I slid my chair back and grabbed the phone, feeling as confused as Ruth looked. Doris could have radioed me. That would have been procedure. Maybe something was really up in 4708.

"Yeah?" I said.

"Spade," she said—my fannish friends had called me Spade since I solved the first case almost twelve years before—"you've gotta come up here. Now."

"What's going on?" I asked.

"An absolute disaster," she said, and hung up.

"Why didn't she use the radio?" Ruth asked.

I shrugged. "I guess she didn't want anyone else wandering up to the room." I eased myself out of my special chair, the one that I insist a con-com bring to every convention if they want my services, and with a push of a button, shut down the financial files on Dinocon's main computer. Then I made my way slowly—because I never hurry—to the fourth floor of the main convention hotel.

Dinocon had 8,000 registered attendees, and it was only Friday afternoon. The convention was scheduled to go through Sunday, and another 2,000 people were expected at the door on Saturday. Most of these folks were already crowding the halls, having conversations with friends they hadn't seen for a while and trying to discover where that night's parties would be held. I squeezed my way through—negotiating packed hallways was never easy for a man of my bulk—and made it to the elevator in time to nab the last spot. No one complained, though, as I squooshed people toward the back. Part of that was my con-com badge—regular con attendees knew better than to harass a person in a con-com badge—and part of it was my reputation.

"Hey, Spade!" someone yelled from the back. "You get a piece of that diamond?"

"I don't charge for my services," I said, in a gently chiding voice. I made my money years ago as an early employee of Microsoft. I took all my bonuses in stock, and then retired at the age of 31, not as rich as Bill Gates, but rich enough.

"He's a gentleman detective," someone else said from the back, and the entire elevator chuckled.

"Imagine," I said as the doors opened on four, "a gentleman—and a scholar."

I got off, but not before I heard more giggling as the doors closed. Fannish humor was not the stuff of stand-up routines, but it was usually full of sweet, if not always socially adept, affection.

The room 4708 was on what had been designated by the hotel as a party floor. On these floors, it was okay to have loud conversation all night, to serve beer in rooms, and to talk in the hallways. Other floors, the non-party floors, were for people who actually wanted to sleep during the con, something I hadn't done in the last thirteen conventions I had attended.

Photocopied 8"x11" signs were taped onto the wallpaper, most of them announcing bid parties for other conventions. The signs on 4708 looked professionally done on slick glossy paper. They announced the first annual Literature Con to be held in an ancient Hilton an hour outside of Manhattan. I stared at the signs for a moment, frowning. Anyone with half a brain knew that most of Dinocon's attendees weren't likely to attend a literature con, especially one held all the way across the country. But the posters had another draw besides their slick appearance.

Food.

Come to our bid party, the sign read, *and dine at your heart's content. Award-winning chocolates, Lucinda's World Famous Chili, and gourmet dishes from the farthest reaches of the Solar System. Come to* the *party of the convention. You'll talk about it for the next three lifetimes.*

Curiouser and curiouser. Lucinda was Lucinda Danielle Stanhope, also known as the Martha Stewart of Science Fiction. Lucinda hated media cons, thinking that they ruined "pure" science fiction. Pure science fiction, to her, was anything beautifully written with long treatises on science. She thought plot-driven fiction an abomination, and sf on movies and television beneath her notice.

Although she might have changed that opinion, since her current boyfriend, who had started as Science Fiction's answer to James Joyce, had gotten a job as a story consultant for a major studio. ("A guy has to make a buck," he said to me at the last Worldcon. "Besides, since *Independence Day*, everyone is hot for sf properties.")

She might have changed her opinion, but I doubted it.

I had known Lucinda for a long time. She and I had had a run-in at Con Diego (called Con Digeo by its attendees because of all the typos in the program book) several years back and I had tried, unsuccessfully, to avoid her ever since. Our conversations from that day on had consisted of only two words, uttered in passing.

Asshole, she say.

Bitch, I'd respond.

I sighed, squared my shoulders, and braced myself for the verbal onslaught as I knocked on the door.

Doris answered. She looked grim and shaky. She motioned me inside and closed the door.

The suite smelled of fresh bread, chili, and something foul, something I had never smelled before and wasn't sure I wanted to smell again. We stood in an entry that led to the bathroom on the left, a main room just before me, and a bedroom on the right. The security kid so skinny he was skeletal and a shade of green I'd never seen outside of a blacklight poster, leaned against a faux Louis the Fourteenth table. He had a hand over his mouth and was taking deep breaths, as if to calm his stomach.

"What is it?" I asked.

Doris pointed toward the main room. I lumbered in, cautiously, not sure what to expect. A chocolate pterodactyl hung from the ceiling and flower arrangements that looked vaguely prehistoric stood on every end-table, along with cute little origami triceratops heads. A human-sized tyrannosaurus rex made entirely out of cheese stood on a circular mirror stand in the center of the room. Crock pots filled with chili bubbled on a table leaning against the wall dividing the main room from the bathroom.

"What—?" I started to ask again, and then I saw her.

She was sprawled on the floor, her left hand resting on the glass double doors leading out to the patio. The doors were closed. I cautiously made my way around the cheese dinosaur and the main table, still in the middle of preparations for the night's party, and stopped near her apron-clad torso.

There was no doubt it was Lucinda. She wore a linen pantsuit beneath that apron, and in her right hand she held an apple partially julienned into a stegosaurus. It was her head that was the problem.

It had been stomped flat, crushed into unrecognizability. More gray matter than I would have expected spattered the teal carpet, mixed with more blood than I had ever seen in my life. I swallowed twice, hard, not wanting to repeat the pea soup episode and contaminate the crime scene. Then I cautiously made my way back into the foyer.

"You call the cops?" I asked.

"No!" Doris said. "They'd shut us down."

"Damn straight they'd shut us down," I said. "We have a murderer on the loose here."

The kid moaned and headed toward the bathroom.

I grabbed his arm. "Uh-uh," I said. "Puke in the public restroom. You don't want to contaminate a crime scene."

"Too late," he mumbled, yanked free, and stumbled into the bathroom, kicking the door closed behind him.

"Poor kid," Doris said. "I'm amazed he has any stomach left."

"Listen, Doris, we gotta call the cops." I covered my hand with my sleeve and reached for the black rotary dial on the faux Louis the Fourteenth.

Doris put her hand on mine, forcing the receiver down.

"It's Friday afternoon," she said. "Think about what that means."

Eight thousand attendees, all of whom would demand refunds. The hotel, which would sue for breach of contract. The reputation, which would shut down all Los Angeles area conventions for the foreseeable future, not to mention all media cons, not to mention all conventions held in this hotel chain forever.

Millions of dollars, all because Lucinda made someone stomping mad.

"Can't we at least wait until tomorrow?" Doris asked.

Retching sounds echoed from the bathroom. My stomach rolled in sympathy.

"Tomorrow?" I asked. "Don't you remember the party signs that are up all over this convention. For tonight? In this room?"

"Can't we change them to tomorrow night?" she asked. "Then we won't have to refund, and we won't be in breach of contract."

But we would still have the reputation problem, along with another one. "Tampering with a crime scene is illegal, Doris," I said softly.

"Can't you solve this?" she asked. "Can't you solve this before the cops get here?"

"I've never done a murder investigation before, Doris," I said.

"*Please*," she asked. "If we can give them a suspect, they won't shut us down, and Ruth and I can handle the PR problem, at least long enough to save the con."

"You don't care that a woman has been trampled in her own hotel room?"

Doris crossed her muscular arms. "You really need to ask me that, Spade? I wouldn't be so rude as to ask you."

She could have, though. Because I was upset. Lucinda had her points. She made a mean chocolate soufflé, and she knew more about fannish foods than anyone I had ever met. She also had her moments: the charity auction she ran for literacy at Orycon in the early '90s brought in $5,000 more than usual because she browbeat the attendees into spending more money. And she got them to do it by having them buy signed books.

Sometimes I found myself in complete agreement with Lucinda's arguments.

And that terrified me.

I stared at Doris.

"Will you help us?" she asked.

I sighed. "I won't tamper with the crime scene, and I will meet with the police when they arrive. You will call them from this room and you will make sure that no one else enters here. You'll also keep the kid from talking to anyone but me. If I happen to solve this thing before the police arrive, fine. But I won't go any farther than that. I'm not going to let some murderer run loose because you want to hold a media con honoring one of the lamest movies of all time."

"The special effects were cool." The kid had opened the door to the bathroom. He was now a chalk white.

"But the plot sucked," I said. Then I nodded at Doris. "Call. I'm going to snoop a bit. And don't leave until I tell you to. Got that?"

She nodded and reached for the phone. I stopped her. "Cover your hands with your sleeves. And don't touch anything besides that receiver."

She glared at me, but followed my instructions. I prowled into the bedroom, deciding to talk to the kid after his breath cleared up.

Lucinda, not surprisingly, was a neat freak. She had arrived and unpacked, her clothing hanging on her hangers in the walk-in closet. Each item was separated by tissue paper, and her hats were in boxes on the shelf above. Her shoes were lined up below in neat little rows beneath the matching clothes. She had two wigs on the dressing table, one studded with little plastic dinosaurs—the clear brightly colored kind that bartenders used to put in drinks in the mid-sixties. A silver lamé dress hung from the plant hook in the ceiling. Lucinda had planned to go all out on this party, and it surprised me. She had to be doing a favor for someone. Media cons were beneath her—and while she enjoyed fannish cooking, she hated fannish clothing.

I got back into the foyer as Doris hung up the phone. "I didn't tell them it was a murder," she said.

I mentally shook my head. That would be her problem when the cops arrived. It would be better for all of us if I had some idea what had happened.

"Okay, kid," I said to the security boy, "come into my office and talk to me. And don't touch anything."

The kid's color still hadn't returned. He followed me into Lucinda's bedroom and started to close the door.

"Don't touch," I said. We went deep into the bowels of the room, and stopped near the bed. I knew that Doris would have trouble hearing us from this spot because I had had trouble hearing her on the phone.

"What's your name?" I asked.

"Chad," he said. I raised a single eyebrow, Spocklike. I had never met a kid who worked con security named Chad. Or at least, a kid who worked con security who would admit to being named Chad.

"Okay," I said, "I need to know: what made you come to this room in the first place?"

He wiped his mouth with the back of his hand. That stomach of his was amazingly weak. "I was by the flyer table—that was my post—when these fans came down the stairs and told me they'd heard a huge pounding on the fourth floor. They took me to their room on three and I heard it too, like something really heavy was going to crash through the floor. Then I came up here. The door was open, and I let myself in. It was really quiet. I called out to see if anyone was here, and then I saw the food. I went in to grab a snack and—"

He burped, then covered his mouth, swallowing hard. "Sorry," he said.

"It's all right," I said. "Do you know who these fans were?"

"Not by name," he said. "But they have the room below this one."

And were probably preparing for another party since the room below also had to be a suite. I rubbed my chin in proper detective fashion. I had a conundrum. I need to talk to those fans, but I didn't want to leave Doris alone in the room. Nor did I want anyone else to know what had happened to Lucinda.

Then I realized it didn't matter. Doris had been in the room without me already. I had investigated, and I knew how things looked. I had seen everything but the bathroom, and that could be remedied.

I took the kid back to the foyer. "Wait here," I said, and peered into the bathroom. The kid had already contaminated the crime scene—several times—but there didn't seem to be much to see. The bathtub was still maid-spotless and the counter had Lucinda's make-up and nothing else. The toilet seat was up, one of the towels was askew, and otherwise everything looked fine. It didn't even smell as bad as I thought it would.

"Okay," I said as I emerged. "Let's find those fans. You wait here, Doris, and don't touch anything."

"Don't worry," she said, looking faintly annoyed at the suggestion.

The kid and I slipped into the hallway. The con was filling up. Two women wearing belly dancer skirts and midriff tops, conversed about the proper navel jewel. Five teenage boys compared tattoos. Three grown men, in Klingon boots and armor, adjusted each other's forehead ridges.

The kid and I took the stairs.

The third floor was filled with people in dinosaur costumes. Some were cheap Halloween masks, while others were full-bore papier-mâché or plastic. The costumes looked heavy, they looked hot, and they smelled of glue. I stared at them, mostly at the feet, wondering what kind of pressure a person would need to drive those hard plastic soles through a skull and crush it.

Then we were in front of 3708. The kid knocked on the door. His hand was shaking.

It was opened by a slender woman whose black hair formed perfect Louisa May Alcott ringlets around her face. She wore a lavender satin shirt with purple satin pants, and the outfit somehow looked perfect on her. Her convention badge was clipped to a tiny piece of cardboard inside her shirt's high pocket, so as not to ruin the satin.

"Hi," she said, looking a bit confused.

"Security," the kid said, glancing at me. "Remember? You asked about the big stomping?"

"Oh, yeah." She was staring at me. Her eyes were lavender, like the shirt. I'd never seen eyes like that in person before. Only in photographs of Elizabeth Taylor. "Who're you?"

"I'm from Ops," I said. "Mind if we come in?"

"Why?" She was asking the kid.

"Because when I went upstairs," he said, "I found —"

I kicked him. He shut up.

"He found that he had a few more questions to ask you," I said. "Mind if we come in."

"No," she said. "I guess not."

She got out of our way, and we stepped into the foyer. It exactly matched the suite above, only here the carpet was brown. Two men sat in the suite's living room. They looked vaguely familiar. They stood as they saw us come in.

"Something wrong?" the first one asked.

He was tall and muscular—those fakey kind of muscles that come from too much health club, and too much low-fat food. His shirt was unbuttoned below the navel, revealing a washboard stomach, and his bare feet looked manicured. His companion wore ripped jeans and a *Star Trek* t-shirt, but unless I missed my guess, his hair had been permed.

Interesting look, for fans. It looked a little too Hollywood, a little too put together, for my tastes. Maybe these folks were slumming.

"You guys with the convention?" I asked.

"What's this all about?" T-Shirt asked. He had his hands on his hips. Same fakey muscles, and he didn't look as if he had ever cracked a book. But, I reminded myself, this was a media con. Folks here didn't have to crack books, even though most of them did.

"Of course we're with the convention," the woman said, and tugged gently on her badge as if to prove it.

"What's your interest?" I asked. "Filking?"

"Excuse me," Manicured asked. His face flamed and he looked insulted.

"Fill-king," the kid said, "not fucking."

Interesting comment, I thought, but I didn't look at him. "Pipe down, Chad," I said. "What are you guys doing at the con?"

"Anyone can come," the woman said, apparently realizing that my questions had more importance than the guys were giving them credit for. "Right?"

"Of course," I said, "but usually people have special reasons for attending. What are yours?"

"We like dinosaurs," T-Shirt said.

"Fascinating," I said in my best Spock voice. No one laughed, even though most fans usually did. My best Spock voice was pretty damn good. "So what's your favorite dinosaur? A plugosaurus or a brontodacdyl?"

"All of 'em," T-Shirt said.

"Hmmm," I said. "Hear you had some noise problems."

"Yeah, man, sounded like weird pounding upstairs," Manicured said. "Like someone was trying to punch a hole in the floor."

"Sounds serious," I said. "Will someone move that chair over here?" I pointed to a square wooden chair that seemed to be the sturdiest thing in the room. T-Shirt moved the chair to the place I pointed to, right next to the balcony doors.

"Spot me, Chad, will you?" I asked as I climbed up.

"Ah, um, ah, you might want me to do that," he said.

"No need," I said, even though the chair was groaning under my weight. I reached up and removed the ceiling panel. Gobs of dust and dirt rained on me, and I had to clear a spider web, but after that I had a pretty good glimpse of the space between the ceiling and the floor above.

"Looks normal," I said, and to my surprise, it did. I put the tile back. "You guys are safe."

"That's it?" the woman asked. "That's all? It sounded wretched up there."

"It was," Chad said. I braced myself on his shoulder and squeezed as I got down. It shut him up again.

"That's it," I said cheerfully. "I hope you have a good con."

"Ah, thanks," T-Shirt said. He was frowning at me.

The kid and I left. The dino costumes flooded the hall. The newer ones looked even more realistic than the earlier ones. Especially the Spielbergian velociraptors. All terrifyingly icky except for the guy wearing blue jeans and a tie-dye brontosaurus head. And the inevitable tot dressed as Barney.

One glance at the elevator told me we weren't going back to the fourth floor that way. Too crowded. It also meant the cops wouldn't come up very quickly when they arrived.

"Where to now?" the kid asked.

I didn't answer. I was feeling pretty annoyed with him. Pretty annoyed with the whole thing, really. I wanted to get back to my Ops computer with its lovely numbers and forget I had ever gotten involved with this detecting business.

Even if I was good at it.

We took the stairs and I was puffing by the time we reached the fourth floor. I hadn't had this much exercise in weeks. And I was moving faster than I liked.

Most of the dino costumes were on the third floor. Regular con-goers littered the fourth. None of them looked like the three ringers downstairs.

I shave-and-a-haircut knocked on 4708. Doris answered immediately. "What took you so long?"

I didn't answer. As I came in, I asked, "Did Lucinda know I was coming to Dinocon?"

"How should I know?" Doris asked.

I glared at her.

She sighed, exasperated. "Probably. If she was looking. You would have been hard to miss since your name was in the con-com listing in all the progress reports. Why?"

I had my suspicions. I made my way back into the suite's main room.

"Hey!" the kid said. "What're you doing?"

His voice had gotten increasingly shrill. I ignored him. I made my way to the body, and, just as I remembered, the floor didn't sag under my considerable weight.

I knelt beside the body. The gray matter and blood were drying in a perfect arch.

"Hey!" the kid yelled. "You said no tampering."

"Grab him, Doris," I said through my teeth. He was getting on my nerves. This whole thing was.

I grabbed the right wrist, dislodging the julienned stegosaurus, and felt—plastic. Soft, lifelike, fake plastic.

"Bitch," I mumbled. I half expected the crushed dummy to mumble "asshole" in return. Then, louder, I said, "Doris, did you call 911?"

She didn't answer. I turned. She was frowning at me. "Doris?"

She flushed. "No," she said. "I called the regular line. I wanted to give you as much time as possible."

Her caution had worked to our advantage. "Call and cancel," I said. "Then break that kid's arm if he doesn't tell you where Lucinda is."

"Lucinda —!"

"Just do it." First time I'd ever understood the sense of a Nike ad.

She twisted the kid's arm up behind his back. Within seconds, he was screaming, "Executive Suite! Executive Suite!"

I got up and walked over to him. "Key," I said.

He handed me a specially marked executive floor key. "Come on, Doris," I said. "Keep a good grip on this kid and commandeer us an elevator."

She did exactly as she was told.

***

ON THE WAY UP, I explained the whole thing, and the kid wisely said nothing, confirming all my suspicions. I was trying to contain my anger, because this thing had just become personal.

And to think I would have mourned the bitch if that had truly been her on the floor below.

You see, the plan was simple: the execution was hard. Lucky for Lucinda that her boyfriend had his new job in Hollywood and even luckier for her that most special effects guys are also sf nerds. Ironic that she needed media people to tamper with a media con. But Lucinda had always been a bit dim when it came to irony.

And, apparently, detail, at least non-food related detail.

First there was the fannish clothing. No matter what kind of theme party Lucinda gave, she never, ever dressed in fannish clothes. No wigs decorated with little plastic dinosaurs, no silver lamé dress. She might have consented to work a media con, but she would never have given up her stylishly proper clothing. She planned the perfect media party, all right, down to the clothes, forgetting that she would never, ever wear those clothes because, of course, she didn't plan to.

But that wasn't the only detail that bothered me. The three "fans" on the floor below had been extras in a straight-to-video sf release that I'd been watching at home a few nights before the con. I would have made them as non-skiffy folk anyway. All science fiction fans—media and lit alike—know the difference between a real dinosaur and a made-up one.

And then there was Chad, clearly another actor for hire. Except he overdid the vomit bit, and the bathroom smelled as if the maid had just left. Lucinda probably hadn't counted on the strength of my sniffer.

But she had counted on me. In fact, I had been the center of her plan. Without me, it wouldn't have worked.

She knew that I knew better than to tamper with a crime scene, no matter how great the temptation. She knew that I had a healthy respect for the authorities and that I would insist on cops being present.

And she knew that the cops would see this for the hoax it was. She would appear at the right moment, blame the convention for overreacting to her little party, piss off the cops just enough to get the whole con shut down. The hotel chain would have been angry, the attendees would have demanded refunds, and the whole cascade effect that Doris had foreseen when she first saw that body would have occurred. Media cons, not just in LA, but all over the country would have suffered, and possibly died.

Lucinda's little stunt would have caused more damage than the murder. It was sabotage, served cold.

***

WHEN WE REACHED the executive suite, Doris made the kid open the door. Lucinda saw him, stood up, and cooed. She was dressed for her act in a white sheath that accented her lightly tanned skin and golden hair.

When she saw us, her eyes widened.

"You bitch," Doris said, blowing my line and letting go of the kid. He started to back away, but I shoved him forward and closed the door behind us.

"Back off, Doris," I said. "She's mine. There won't be any cops, Lucinda. You won't ruin this convention."

"I'm going to see that you're banned from cons for-ever. I'm going to make sure that your name is taken out of the Fannish Directory. I'm going to—"

"For what? For a little party I planned to throw for some friends?" Lucinda asked. "Don't you think it rather cute? I do."

"You—"

Doris lunged for her, and I caught her, staggering a bit under her power. The kid bee-lined for the bath-room, fear making his intentions real this time.

"Go to Ops," I said to Doris. "Tell them everything is fine. I can take it from here."

"I'm going to get you," Doris said, but she listened to me. She knew as well as I did that strange things hap-pened at sf conventions, and that there was no proving malicious intent here.

Knowing about it was something else.

"Misunderstandings are so tragic, Doris," Lucinda said, blinking her blue eyes guilelessly.

Doris growled and disappeared out the door. I stood in front of Lucinda. "Media cons aren't your style."

She smiled. It was sweet as rhubarb pie. "They're not yours either."

"I don't see anything wrong with people having fun. I'm a bit more open-minded than you, Lucinda. I believe people can enjoy reading and watching movies. I believe there's room in fandom for both."

"You're so naive," she said. "These cons are so anti-literature. They appeal only to the ignorant.

People who don't understand real science, or real science fiction."

"I think people who think they guard pure science fiction may not understand real science or real science fiction either," I said pointedly.

"Good god," she said, "a philosophical discussion when I have a party to finish."

"It seems strange to me that you'd put on a party here, Lucinda."

She shrugged. "I thought I'd give these people the opportunity to come to a lit-con and see what they were missing."

"So kind of you," I said.

She smoothed her dress. "We all do what we can in the circumstances provided."

At that moment, I almost told her what tripped her up. I almost told her that it was her lack of scientific knowledge, her lack of understanding of forensic science that had destroyed her. First, the splatter had been too pretty, too uniform. Second, and more importantly, the type of force it took to stomp out someone's brains would have caused damage to the plywood floor. Damage someone of my weight would have felt in loose boards or groaning wood.

But I didn't. Why give her the ammunition? She might try again someday.

"Am I excused?" she asked brightly.

"There is no excuse for you, Lucinda," I said in my best fannish manner, and moved out of her way.

***

THE BANE OF THE NON-LICENSED INVESTIGATOR is that we have no real authority. We can't arrest. Worse yet, people with authority often look down their noses at us.

So we are forced to take some matters into our own hands.

Lucinda, misguided as she was, was clever. Who could prove that the panic the kid, Doris, and I felt was anything more than a product of our own imaginations? She would say that she had planned a perfect party, and we had nearly ruined it.

In fact, that night, she did carry off the party with full aplomb. She did change the victim from her clone to that of a lawyer, in keeping with *Jurassic Park* (the movie) tradition, and she did pour ice in the bathtub, but those were the only changes she made. The party was the hit of the convention, and became the talk of sf—both media- and literature-oriented—for years to come. It was, in its own way, the Woodstock of science fiction. Eventually everyone who was anyone claimed they had been there, even if they had been clear across the country at the time.

Everyone who was anyone except me.

You see, I was in Ops, checking the computer records. We had an unexplained power failure just as I was transferring Lucinda's credit card information from her con file into an active file so that we could bill her account.

Unfortunately, the accident caused blips in her credit record that cascaded down the system and destroyed her credit rating for the next year. She had to defend and deny and repair, all of which took time away from cons and con parties, and fandom.

And somehow she got it in her pretty little head that this would happen again if she ever attempted to sabotage—even accidentally—a major convention again.

Misunderstandings are so tragic.

But we all do what we can in the circumstances provided.

G-Men

"There's something addicting about a secret."
—J. Edgar Hoover

THE SQUALID LITTLE ALLEY smelled of piss. Detective Seamus O'Reilly tugged his overcoat closed and wished he'd worn boots. He could feel the chill of his metal flashlight through the worn glove on his right hand.

Two beat cops stood in front of the bodies, and the coroner crouched over them. His assistant was already setting up the gurneys, body bags draped over his arm. The coroner's van had blocked the alley's entrance, only a few yards away.

O'Reilly's partner, Joseph McKinnon, followed him. McKinnon had trained his own flashlight on the fire escapes above, unintentionally alerting any residents to the police presence.

But they probably already knew. Shootings in this part of the city were common. The neighborhood teetered between swank and corrupt. Far enough from

Central Park for degenerates and muggers to use the alleys as corridors, and, conversely, close enough for new money to want to live with a peak of the city's most famous expanse of green.

The coroner, Thomas Brunner, had set up two expensive, battery-operated lights on garbage can lids placed on top of the dirty ice, one at the top of the bodies, the other near the feet. O'Reilly crouched so he wouldn't create any more shadows.

"What've we got?" he asked.

"Dunno yet." Brunner was using his gloved hands to part the hair on the back of the nearest corpse's skull. "It could be one of those nights."

O'Reilly had worked with Brunner for eighteen years now, since they both got back from the war, and he hated it when Brunner said it could be one of those nights. That meant the corpses would stack up, which was usually a summer thing, but almost never happened in the middle of winter.

"Why?" O'Reilly asked. "What else we got?"

"Some colored limo driver shot two blocks from here." Brunner was still parting the hair. It took O'Reilly a minute to realize it was matted with blood. "And two white guys pulled out of their cars and shot about four blocks from that."

O'Reilly felt a shiver run through him that had nothing to do with the cold. "You think the shootings are related?"

"Dunno," Brunner said. "But I think it's odd, don't you? Five dead in the space of an hour, all in a six-block radius."

O'Reilly closed his eyes for a moment. Two white guys pulled out of their cars, one Negro driver of a limo, and now two white guys in an alley. Maybe they were related, maybe they weren't.

He opened his eyes, then wished he hadn't. Brunner had his finger inside a bullet hole, a quick way to judge caliber.

"Same type of bullet," Brunner said.

"You handled the other shootings?"

"I was on scene with the driver when some fag called this one in."

O'Reilly looked at Brunner. Eighteen years, and he still wasn't used to the man's casual bigotry.

"How did you know the guy was queer?" O'Reilly asked. "You talk to him?"

"Didn't have to." Brunner nodded toward the building in front of them. "Weekly party for degenerates in the penthouse apartment every Thursday night. Thought you knew."

O'Reilly looked up. Now he understood why McKinnon had been shining his flashlight at the upper story windows. McKinnon had worked vice before he got promoted to homicide.

"Why would I know?" O'Reilly said.

McKinnon was the one who answered. "Because of the standing orders."

"I'm not playing twenty questions," O'Reilly said. "I don't know about a party in this building and I don't know about standing orders."

"The standing orders are," McKinnon said as if he were an elementary school teacher, "not to bust it, no matter what kind of lead you got. You see someone go in, you forget about it. You see someone come out, you avert your eyes. You complain, you get moved to a different shift, maybe a different precinct."

"Jesus." O'Reilly was too far below to see if there was any movement against the glass in the penthouse suite. But whoever lived there—whoever partied there—had learned to shut off the lights before the cops arrived.

"Shot in the back of the head," Brunner said before O'Reilly could process all of the information. "That's just damn strange."

O'Reilly looked at the corpses—really looked at them—for the first time. Two men, both rather heavy set. Their faces were gone, probably splattered all over the walls. Gloved hands, nice shoes, one of them wearing a white scarf that caught the light.

Brunner had to search for the wound in the back of the head, which made that the entry point. The exit wounds had destroyed the faces.

O'Reilly looked behind him. No door on that building, but there was one on the building where the party was held. If they'd been exiting the building and were surprised by a queer basher or a mugger, they'd've been shot in the front, not the back.

"How many times were they shot?" O'Reilly asked.

"Looks like just the once. Large caliber, close range. I'd say it was a purposeful headshot, designed to do maximum damage." Brunner felt the back of the closest corpse. "There doesn't seem to be anything on the torso."

"They still got their wallets?" McKinnon asked.

"Haven't checked yet." Brunner reached into the back pants pocket of the corpse he'd been searching and clearly found nothing. So he grabbed the front of the overcoat and reached inside.

He removed a long thin wallet—old fashioned, the kind made for the larger bills of forty years before. Hand-tailored, beautifully made.

These men weren't hurting for money.

Brunner handed the wallet to O'Reilly, who opened it. And stopped when he saw the badge inside. His mouth went dry.

"We got a feebee," he said, his voice sounding strangled.

"What?" McKinnon asked.

"FBI," Brunner said dryly. McKinnon had only moved to homicide the year before. Vice rarely had to deal with FBI. Homicide did only on sensational cases. O'Reilly could count on one hand the number of times he'd spoken to agents in the New York bureau.

"Not just any feebee either," O'Reilly said. "The Associate Director. Clyde A. Tolson."

McKinnon whistled. "Who's the other guy?"

This time, O'Reilly did the search. The other corpse, the heavier of the two, also smelled faintly of perfume. This man had kept his wallet in the inner pocket of his suit coat, just like his companion had.

O'Reilly opened the wallet. Another badge, just like he expected. But he didn't expect the bulldog face glaring at him from the wallet's interior.

Nor had he expected the name.

"Jesus, Mary and Joseph," he said.

"What've we got?" McKinnon asked.

O'Reilly handed him the wallet, opened to the slim paper identification.

"The Director of the FBI," he said, his voice shaking. "Public Hero Number One. J. Edgar Hoover."

***

FRANCIS XAVIER BRYCE—Frank to his friends, what few of them he still had left—had just dropped off to sleep when the phone rang. He cursed, caught himself, apologized to Mary, and then remembered she wasn't there.

The phone rang again and he fumbled for the light, knocking over the highball glass he'd used to mix his mom's recipe for sleepless nights, hot milk, butter and honey. It turned out that, at the tender age of 36, hot milk and butter laced with honey wasn't a recipe for sleep; it was a recipe for heartburn.

And for a smelly carpet if he didn't clean the mess up.

He found the phone before he found the light.

"What?" he snapped.

"You live near Central Park, right?" A voice he didn't recognize, but one that was clearly official, asked the question without a hello or an introduction.

"More or less." Bryce rarely talked about his apartment. His parents had left it to him and, as his wife was fond of sniping, it was too fancy for a junior G-Man.

The voice rattled off an address. "How far is that from you?"

"About five minutes." If he didn't clean up the mess on the floor. If he spent thirty seconds pulling on the clothes he'd piled onto the chair beside the bed.

"Get there. Now. We got a situation."

"What about my partner?" Bryce's partner lived in Queens.

"You'll have back-up. You just have to get to the scene. The moment you get there, you shut it down."

"Um." Bryce hated sounding uncertain, but he had no choice. "First, sir, I need to know who I'm talking to. Then I need to know what I'll find."

"You'll find a double homicide. And you're talking to Eugene Hart, the Special Agent in Charge. I shouldn't have to identify myself to you."

Now that he had, Bryce recognized Hart's voice. "Sorry, sir. It's just procedure."

"Fuck procedure. Take over that scene. *Now*."

"Yes, sir," Bryce said, but he was talking into an empty phone line. He hung up, hands shaking, wishing he had some BromoSeltzer.

He'd just come off a long, messy investigation of another agent. Walter Cain had been about to get married when he remembered he had to inform the Bureau of that fact and, as per regulation, get his bride vetted before walking down the aisle.

Bryce had been the one to investigate the future Mrs. Cain, and had been the one to find out about her rather seamy past—two Vice convictions under a different name, and one hospitalization after a rather messy backstreet abortion. Turned out Cain knew about his future wife's past, but the Bureau hadn't liked it.

And two nights ago, Bryce had to be the one to tell Cain that he couldn't marry his now-reformed, somewhat religious, beloved. The soon-to-be Mrs. Cain had taken the news hard. She had gone to Bellevue this afternoon after slashing her wrists.

And Bryce had been the one to tell Cain what his former fiancée had done. Just a few hours ago.

Sometimes Bryce hated this job.

Despite his orders, he went into the bathroom, soaked one of Mary's precious company towels in water, and dropped the thing on the spilled milk. Then he pulled on his clothes, and finger-combed his hair.

He was a mess—certainly not the perfect representative of the Bureau. His white shirt was stained with marinara from that night's take-out, and his tie wouldn't keep a crisp knot. The crease had long since left his trousers and his shoes hadn't been shined in weeks. Still, he grabbed his black overcoat, hoping it would hide everything.

He let himself out of the apartment before he remembered the required and much hated hat, went back inside, grabbed the hat as well as his gun and his identification.

Jesus, he was tired. He hadn't slept since Mary walked out. Mary, who had been vetted by the FBI and who had passed with flying colors. Mary, who had turned out to be more of a liability than any former hooker ever could have been.

And now, because of her, he was heading toward something big, and he was one-tenth as sharp as usual.

All he could hope for was that the SAC had overreacted. And he had a hunch—a two in the morning, get-your-ass-over-there-now hunch—that the SAC hadn't overreacted at all.

***

ATTORNEY GENERAL ROBERT F. KENNEDY sat in his favorite chair near the fire in his library. The house was quiet even though his wife and eight children were asleep upstairs. Outside, the rolling landscape was covered in a light dusting of snow—rare for McLean, Virginia even at this time of year.

He held a book in his left hand, his finger marking the spot. The Greeks had comforted him in the few months since Jack died, but lately Kennedy had discovered Camus.

He had been about to copy a passage into his notebook when the phone rang. At first he sighed, feeling all of the exhaustion that had weighed on him since the assassination. He didn't want to answer the phone. He didn't want to be bothered—not now, not ever again.

But this was the direct line from the White House and if he didn't answer it, someone else in the house would.

He set the Camus book face down on his chair and crossed to the desk before the third ring. He answered with a curt, "Yes?"

"Attorney General Kennedy, sir?" The voice on the other end sounded urgent. The voice sounded familiar to him even though he couldn't place it.

"Yes?"

"This is Special Agent John Haskell. You asked me to contact you, sir, if I heard anything important about Director Hoover, no matter what the time."

Kennedy leaned against the desk. He had made that request back when his brother had been president, back when Kennedy had been the first attorney general since the 1920s who actually demanded accountability from Hoover.

Since Lyndon Johnson had taken over the presidency, accountability had gone by the wayside. These days Hoover rarely returned Kennedy's phone calls.

"Yes, I did tell you that," Kennedy said, resisting the urge to add, but *I don't care about that old man any longer.*

"Sir, there are rumors—credible ones—that Director Hoover has died in New York."

Kennedy froze. For a moment, he flashed back to that unseasonably warm afternoon when he'd sat just outside with the federal attorney for New York City, Robert Morganthau and the chief of Morganthau's criminal division, Silvio Mollo, talking about prosecuting various organized crime figures.

Kennedy could still remember the glint of the sunlight on the swimming pool, the taste of the tuna fish sandwich Ethel had brought him, the way the men—despite their topic—had seemed lighthearted.

Then the phone rang, and J. Edgar Hoover was on the line. Kennedy almost didn't take the call, but he did and Hoover's cold voice said, *I have news for you. The President's been shot.*

Kennedy had always disliked Hoover, but since that day, that awful day in the bright sunshine, he hated that fat bastard. Not once—not in that call, not in the subsequent calls—did Hoover express condolences or show a shred of human concern.

"Credible rumors?" Kennedy repeated, knowing he probably sounded as cold as Hoover had three months ago, and not caring. He'd chosen Haskell as his liaison precisely because the man didn't like Hoover either. Kennedy had needed someone inside Hoover's hierarchy, unbeknownst to Hoover, which was difficult since Hoover kept his hand in everything. Haskell was one of the few who fit the bill.

"Yes, sir, quite credible."

"Then why haven't I received official contact?"

"I'm not even sure the President knows, sir."

Kennedy leaned against the desk. "Why not, if the rumors are credible?"

"Um, because, sir, um, it seems Associate Director Tolson was also shot, and um, they were, um, in a rather suspect area."

Kennedy closed his eyes. All of Washington knew that Tolson was the closest thing Hoover had to a wife. The two old men had been life-long companions. Even though they didn't live together, they had every meal together. Tolson had been Hoover's hatchet man until the last year or so, when Tolson's health hadn't permitted it.

Then a word Haskell used sank in. "You said shot."

"Yes, sir."

"Is Tolson dead too then?"

"And three other people in the neighborhood," Haskell said.

"My God." Kennedy ran a hand over his face. "But they think this is personal?"

"Yes, sir."

"Because of the location of the shooting?"

"Yes, sir. It seems there was an exclusive gathering in a nearby building. You know the type, sir."

Kennedy didn't know the type—at least not through personal experience. But he'd heard of places like that, where the rich, famous and deviant could spend time with each other, and do whatever it was they liked to do in something approaching privacy.

"So," he said, "the bureau's trying to figure out how to cover this up."

"Or at least contain it, sir."

Without Hoover or Tolson. No one in the bureau was gong to know what to do.

Kennedy's hand started to shake. "What about the files?"

"Files, sir?"

"Hoover's confidential files. Has anyone secured them?"

"Not yet, sir. But I'm sure someone has called Miss Gandy."

Helen Gandy was Hoover's long-time secretary. She had been his right hand as long as Tolson had operated that hatchet.

"So procedure's being followed," Kennedy said, then frowned. If procedure were being followed, shouldn't the acting head of the bureau be calling him?

"No, sir. But the Director put some private instructions in place should he be killed or incapacitated. Private emergency instructions. And those involve letting Miss Gandy know before anyone else."

Even me, Kennedy thought. *Hoover's nominal boss.* "She's not there yet, right?"

"No, sir."

"Do you know where those files are?" Kennedy asked, trying not to let desperation into his voice.

"I've made it my business to know, sir." There was a pause and then Haskell lowered his voice. "They're in Miss Gandy's office, sir."

Not Hoover's like everyone thought. For the first time in months, Kennedy felt a glimmer of hope. "Secure those files."

"Sir?"

"Do whatever it takes. I want them out of there, and I want someone to secure Hoover's house too. I'm acting on the orders of the President. If anyone tells you that they are doing the same, they're mistaken. The President made his wishes clear on this point. He often said if anything happens to that old queer—" And here Kennedy deliberately used LBJ's favorite phrase for Hoover "—then we need those files before they can get into the wrong hands."

"I'm on it, sir."

"I can't stress to you the importance of this," Kennedy said. In fact, he couldn't talk about the importance at all. Those files could ruin his brother's legacy. The secrets in there could bring down Kennedy too, and his entire family.

"And if the rumors about the Director's death are wrong, sir?"

Kennedy felt a shiver of fear. "Are they?"

"I seriously doubt it."

"Then let me worry about that."

And about what LBJ would do when he found out. Because the president upon whose orders Kennedy acted wasn't the current one. Kennedy was following the orders of the only man he believed should be president at the moment.

His brother, Jack.

***

THE SCENE WASN'T HARD TO FIND; a coroner's van blocked the entrance to the alley. Bryce walked quickly, already cold, his heartburn worse than it had been when he had gone to bed.

The neighborhood was in transition. An urban renewal project had knocked down some wonderful turn of the century buildings that had become eyesores. But so far, the buildings that had replaced them were the worst kind of modern—all planes and angles and white with few windows.

In the buildings closest to the park, the lights worked and the streets looked safe. But here, on a side street not far from the construction, the city's shady side showed. The dirty snow was piled against the curb, the streets were dark, and nothing seemed inhabited except that alley with the coroner's van blocking the entrance.

The coroner's van and at least one unmarked car. No press, which surprised him. He shoved his gloved hands in the pockets of his overcoat even though it was against FBI dress code, and slipped between the van and the wall of a grimy brick building.

The alley smelled of old urine and fresh blood. Two beat cops blocked his way until he showed identification. Then, like people usually did, they parted as if he could burn them.

The bodies had fallen side by side in the center of the alley. They looked posed, with their arms up, their legs in classic P position—one leg bent, the other straight. They looked like they could fit perfectly on the dead body diagrams the FBI used to put out in the 1930s. He wondered if they had fallen like this or if this had been the result of the coroner's tampering.

The coroner had messed with other parts of the crime scene—if, indeed, he had been the one who put the garbage can lids on the ice and set battery-powered lamps on them. The warmth of the lamps was melting the ice and sending runnels of water into a nearby grate.

"I hope to hell someone thought to photograph the scene before you melted it," he said.

The coroner and the two cops who had been crouching beside the bodies stood up guiltily. The coroner looked at the garbage can lids and closed his eyes. Then he took a deep breath, opened them, and snapped his fingers at the assistant who was waiting beside a gurney.

"Camera," he said.

"That's Crime Scene's—." the assistant began, then saw everyone looking at him. He glanced at the van. "Never mind."

He walked behind the bodies, further disturbing the scene. Bryce's mouth thinned in irritation. The cops who stood were in plain clothes.

"Detectives," Bryce said, holding his identification, "Special Agent Frank Bryce of the FBI. I've been told to secure this scene. More of my people will be here shortly."

He hoped that last was true. He had no idea who was coming or when they would arrive.

"Good," said the younger detective, a tall man with broad shoulders and an all-American jaw. "The sooner we get out of here the better."

Bryce had never gotten that reaction from a detective before. Usually the detectives were territorial, always reminding him that this was New York City and that the scene belonged to them.

The other detective, older, face grizzled by time and work, held out his gloved hand. "Forgive my partner's rudeness. I'm Seamus O'Reilly. He's Joseph McAllister and we'll help you in any way we can."

"I appreciate it," Bryce said, taking O'Reilly's hand and shaking it. "I guess the first thing you can do is tell me what we've got."

"A hell of a mess, that's for sure," said McAllister. "You'll understand when…."

His voice trailed off as his partner took out two long, old-fashioned wallets and handed them to Bryce.

Bryce took them, feeling confused. Then he opened the first, saw the familiar badge, and felt his breath catch. Two FBI agents, in this alley? Shot side-by-side? He looked up, saw the darkened windows.

There used to be rumors about this neighborhood. Some exclusive private sex parties used to be held here, and his old partner had always wanted to visit one just to see if it was a hotbed of Communists like some of the agents had claimed. Bryce had begged off. He was an investigator, not a voyeur.

The two detectives were staring at him, as if they expected more from him. He still had the wallet open in his hand. If the dead men were New York agents, he would know them. He hated solving the deaths of people he knew.

But he steeled himself, looked at the identification, and felt the blood leave his face. His skin grew cold and for a moment he felt lightheaded.

"No," he said.

The detectives still stared at him.

He swallowed. "Have you done a visual i.d.?"

Hoover was recognizable. His picture was on everything. Sometimes Bryce thought Hoover was more famous than the president—any president. He'd certainly been in power longer.

"Faces are gone," O'Reilly said.

"Exit wounds," the coroner added from beside the bodies. His assistant had returned and was taking pictures, the flash showing just how much melt had happened since the coroner arrived.

"Shot in the back of the head?" Bryce blinked. He was tired and his brain was working slowly, but something about the shots didn't match with the body positions.

"If they came out that door," O'Reilly said as he indicated a dark metal door almost hidden in the side of the brick building, "then the shooters had to be waiting beside it."

"Your crime scene people haven't arrived yet, I take it?" Bryce asked.

"No," the coroner said. "They think it's a fag kill. They'll get here when they get here."

Bryce clenched his left fist and had to remind himself to let the fingers loose.

O'Reilly saw the reaction. "Sorry about that," he said, shooting a glare at the coroner. "I'm sure the director was here on business."

Funny business. But Bryce didn't say that. The rumors about Hoover had been around since Bryce joined the FBI just after the war. Hoover quashed them, like he quashed any criticism, but it seemed like the criticism got made, no matter what.

Bryce opened the other wallet, but he already had a guess as to who was beside Hoover, and his guess turned out to be right.

"You want to tell me why your crime scene people believe this is a homosexual killing?" Bryce asked, trying not to let what Mary called his FBI tone into his voice. If Hoover was still alive and this was some kind of plant, Hoover would want to crush the source of this assumption. Bryce would make sure that the source was worth pursuing before going any farther.

"Neighborhood, mostly," McAllister said. "There're a couple of bars, mostly high-end. You have to know someone to get in. Then there's the party, held every week upstairs. Some of the most important men in the city show up at it, or so they used to say in Vice when they told us to stay away."

Bryce nodded, letting it go at that.

"We need your crime scene people here ASAP, and a lot more cops so that we can protect what's left of this scene, in case these men turn out to be who their identification says they are. You search the bodies to see if this was the only identification on them?"

O'Reilly started. He clearly hadn't thought of that. Probably had been too shocked by the first wallets that he found.

The younger detective had already gone back to the bodies. The coroner put out a hand, and did the searching himself.

"You think this was a plant?" O'Reilly asked.

"I don't know what to think," Bryce said. "I'm not here to think. I'm here to make sure everything goes smoothly."

And to make sure the case goes to the FBI. Those words hung unspoken between the two of them. Not that O'Reilly objected, and now Bryce could understand why. This case would be a political nightmare, and no good detective wanted to be in the middle of it.

"How come there's no press?" Bryce asked O'Reilly. "You manage to get rid of them somehow?"

"Fag kill," the coroner said.

Bryce was getting tired of those words. His fist had clenched again, and he had to work at unclenching it.

"Ignore him," O'Reilly said softly. "He's an asshole and the best coroner in the city."

"I heard that," the coroner said affably. "There's no other identification on either of them."

O'Reilly's shoulders slumped, as if he'd been hoping for a different outcome. Bryce should have been hoping as well, but he hadn't been. He had known that Hoover was in town. The entire New York bureau knew, since Hoover always took it over when he arrived—breezing in, giving instructions, making sure everything was just the way he wanted it.

"Before this gets too complicated," O'Reilly said, "you want to see the other bodies?"

"Other bodies?" Bryce felt numb. He could use some caffeine now, but Hoover had ordered agents not to drink coffee on the job. Getting coffee now felt almost disrespectful.

"We got three more." O'Reilly took a deep breath. "And just before you arrived, I got word that they're agents too."

***

SPECIAL AGENT JOHN HASKELL had just installed six of his best agents outside the Director's suite of offices when a small woman showed up, key clutched in her gloved right hand. Helen Gandy, the Director's secretary, looked up at Haskell with the coldest stare he'd ever seen outside of the Director's.

"May I go into my office, Agent Haskell?" Her voice was just as cold. She didn't look upset, and if he hadn't known that she never stayed past five unless directed by Hoover himself, Haskell would have thought she was coming back from a prolonged work break.

"I'm sorry, Ma'am," he said. "No one is allowed inside. President's orders."

"Really?" God, that voice was chilling. He remembered the first time he'd heard it, when he'd been brought to this suite of offices as a brand-new agent, after getting his "Meet the Boss" training before his introduction to the Director. She'd frightened him more than Hoover had.

"Yes, Ma'am. The President says no one can enter."

"Surely he didn't mean me."

Surely he did. But Haskell bit the comment back. "I'm sorry, Ma'am."

"I have a few personal items that I'd like to get, if you don't mind. And the Director instructed me that in the case of…" and for the first time she paused. Her voice didn't break nor did she clear her throat. But she seemed to need a moment to gather herself. "In case of emergency, I was to remove some of his personal items as well."

"If you could tell me what they are, Ma'am, I'll get them."

Her eyes narrowed. "The Director doesn't like others to touch his possessions."

"I'm sorry, Ma'am," he said gently. "But I don't think that matters any longer."

Any other woman would have broken down. After all, she had worked for the old man for forty-five years, side-by-side, every day. Never marrying, not because they had a relationship—Helen Gandy, more than anyone, probably knew the truth behind the Director's relationship with the Associate Director—but because for Helen Gandy, just like for the Director himself, the FBI was her entire life.

"It matters," she said. "Now if you'll excuse me…"

She tried to wriggle past him. She was wiry and stronger than he expected. He had to put out an arm to block her.

"Ma'am," he said in the gentlest tone he could summon, "the President's orders supersede the Director's."

How often had he wanted to say that over the years? How often had he wanted to remind everyone in the Bureau that the President led the Free World, not J. Edgar Hoover.

"In this instance," she snapped, "they do not."

"Ma'am, I'd hate to have some agents restrain you." Although he wasn't sure about that. She had never been nice to him or to anyone he knew. She'd always been sharp or rude. "You're distraught."

"I am not." She clipped each word.

"You are because I say you are, Ma'am."

She raised her chin. For a moment, he thought she hadn't understood. But she finally did.

The balance of power had shifted. At the moment, it was on his side.

"Do I have to call the president then to get my personal effects?" she asked.

But they both knew she wasn't talking about her personal things. And the President was smart enough to know that as well. As hungry to get those files as the Attorney General had seemed despite his Eastern reserve, the President would be utterly ravenous. He wouldn't let some old skirt, as he'd been known to call Miss Gandy, get in his way.

"Go ahead," Haskell said. "Feel free to use the phone in the office across the hall."

She glared at him, then turned on one foot and marched down the corridor. But she didn't head toward a phone—at least not one he could see.

He wondered who she would call. The President wouldn't listen. The Attorney General had issued the order in the president's name. Maybe she would contact one of Hoover's Assistant Directors, the four or five men that Hoover had in his pocket.

Haskell had been waiting for them. But word still hadn't spread through the Bureau. The only reason he knew was because he'd received a call from the SAC of the New York office. New York hated the Director, mostly because the old man went there so often and harassed them.

Someone had probably figured out that there was a crisis from the moment that Haskell had brought his people in to secure the Director's suite. But no one would know that the Director was dead until Miss Gandy made the calls or until someone in the Bureau started along the chain of command—the one designated in the book Hoover had written all those years ago.

Haskell crossed his arms. Sometimes he wished he hadn't let the A.G. know how he felt about the Director. Sometimes he wished he were still a humble assistant, the man who had joined the FBI because he wanted to be a top cop like his hero J. Edgar Hoover.

A man who, it turned out, never made a real arrest or fired a gun or even understood investigation.

There was a lot to admire about the Director—no matter what you said, he'd built a hell of an agency almost from scratch—but he wasn't the man his press made him out to be.

And that was the source of Haskell's disillusionment. He'd wanted to be a top cop. Instead, he snooped into homes and businesses and sometimes even investigated fairly blameless people, looking for a mistake in their past.

Since he'd been transferred to FBIHQ, he hadn't done any real investigating at all. His arrests had slowed, his cases dwindled.

And he'd found himself investigating his boss, trying to find out where the legend ended and the man began. Once he realized that the old man was just a bureaucrat who had learned where all the bodies were buried and used that to make everyone bow to his bidding, Haskell was ripe for the undercover work the A.G. had asked him to do.

Only now he wasn't undercover any more. Now he was standing in the open before the Director's cache of secrets, on the President's orders, hoping that no one would call his bluff.

***

As O'Reilly led him to the limousine, Bryce surreptitiously checked his watch. He'd already been on scene for half an hour, and no back-up had arrived. If he was supposed to secure everything and chase off the NYPD, he'd need some manpower.

But for now, he wanted to see the extent of the problem. The night had gotten colder, and this street was even darker than the street he'd walked down. All of the streetlights were out. The only light came from some porch bulbs above a few entrances. He could barely make out the limousine at the end of the block, and then only because he could see the shadowy forms of the two beat cops standing at the scene, their squad cars parking the limo in.

As he got closer, he recognized the shape of the limo. It was thicker than most limos and rode lower to the ground because it was encased in an extra frame, making it bulletproof. Supposedly, the glass would all be bulletproof as well.

"You said the driver was shot inside the limo?" Bryce asked.

"That's what they told me," O'Reilly said. "I wasn't called to this scene. We were brought in because of the two men in the alley. Even then we were called late."

Bryce nodded. He remembered the coroner's bigotry. "Is that standard procedure for cases involving minorities?"

O'Reilly gave him a sideways glance. Bryce couldn't read O'Reilly's expression in the dark.

"We're overtaxed," O'Reilly said after a moment. "Some cases don't get the kind of treatment they deserve."

"Limo drivers," Bryce said.

"If he'd been killed in the parking garage under the Plaza maybe," O'Reilly said. "But not because of who he was. But because of where he was."

Bryce nodded. He knew how the world worked. He didn't like it. He spoke up against it too many times, which was why he was on shaky ground at the Bureau.

Then his already upset stomach clenched. Maybe he wasn't going to get back-up. Maybe they'd put him on his own here to claim he'd botched the investigation, so that they would be able to cover it up.

He couldn't concentrate on that now. What he had to do was take good notes, make the best case he could, and keep a copy of every damn thing—maybe in more than one place.

"You were called in because of the possibility that the men in the alley could be important," Bryce said.

"That's my guess," O'Reilly said.

"What about the others down the block? Has anyone taken those cases?"

"Probably not," O'Reilly said. "Those bars, you know. It's department policy. The coroner checks bodies in the suspect area, and decides, based on...um...evidence of...um...

activity...whether or not to bring in detectives."

Bryce frowned. He almost asked what the coroner was checking for when he figured out that it was evidence on the body itself, evidence not of the crime, but of certain kinds of sex acts. If that evidence was present, apparently no one thought it worthwhile to investigate the crime.

"You'd think the city would revise that," Bryce said. "A lot of people live dual lives—productive and interesting people."

"Yeah," O'Reilly said. "You'd think. Especially after tonight."

Bryce grinned. He was liking this grizzled cop more and more.

O'Reilly spoke to the beat cops, then motioned Bryce to the limo. As Bryce approached, O'Reilly trained his flashlight on the driver's side.

The window wasn't broken like Bryce had expected. It had been rolled down.

"You got here one James Crawford," said one of the beat cops. "He got identification says he's a feebee, but I ain't never heard of no colored feebee."

"There's only four," Bryce said dryly. And they all worked for Hoover as his personal housekeepers or drivers. "Can I see that identification?"

The beat cop handed him a wallet that matched the ones on Tolson and Hoover. Inside was a badge and identification for James Crawford as well as family photographs. Neither Tolson nor Hoover had had any photographs in their wallets.

Bryce motioned O'Reilly to move a little closer to the body. The head was tilted toward the window. The right side of the skull was gone, the hair glistening with drying blood. With one gloved finger, Bryce pushed the head upright. A single entrance wound above the left ear had caused the damage.

"Brunner says the shots are the same caliber," O'Reilly said.

It took Bryce a moment to realize that Brunner was the coroner.

Bryce carefully searched Crawford but didn't find the man's weapon. Nor could he find a holster or any way to carry a weapon.

"It looks like he wasn't carrying a weapon," Bryce said.

"Neither were the two in the alley," O'Reilly said, and Bryce appreciated his caution in not identifying the other two corpses. "You'd think they would have been."

Bryce shook his head. "They were known for not carrying weapons. But you'd think their driver would have one."

"Maybe they had protection," O'Reilly said.

And Bryce's mouth went dry. Of course they did. The office always joked about who would get HooverWatch on each trip. He'd had to do it a few times.

Agents on HooverWatch followed strict rules, like everything else with Hoover. Remain close enough to see the men entering and exiting an area, stop any suspicious characters, and yet somehow remain inconspicuous.

"You said there were two others shot?"

"Yeah. A block or so from here." O'Reilly waved a hand vaguely down the street.

"Pulled out of one car or two?"

"Not my case," O'Reilly said.

"Two," said the beat cop. "Black sedans. Could barely see them on this cruddy street."

HooverWatch. Bryce swallowed hard, that bile back. Of course. He probably knew the men who were shot.

"Let's look," he said. "You two, make sure the coroner's man photographs this scene before he leaves."

"Yessir," said the second beat cop. He hadn't spoken before.

"And don't let anyone near this scene unless I give the o.k.," Bryce said.

"How come this guy's in charge?" the talkative beat cop asked O'Reilly.

O'Reilly grinned. "Because he's a feebee."

"I'm sorry," the beat cop said automatically turning to Bryce. "I didn't know, sir."

Feebee was an insult—or at least some in the Bureau thought so. Bryce didn't mind it. Any more than he minded when some rookie said "Sack" when he meant "Ess-Ay-Cee." Shorthand worked, sometimes better than people wanted it to.

"Point me in the right direction," he said to the talkative cop.

The cop nodded south. "One block down, sir. You can't miss it. We got guys on those scenes too, but we weren't so sure it was important. You know. We coulda missed stuff."

In other words, they hadn't buttoned up the scene immediately. They'd waited for the coroner to make his verdict, and he probably hadn't, not with the three new corpses nearby.

Bryce took one last look at James Crawford. The man had rolled down his window, despite the cold, and in a bad section of town.

He leaned forward. Underneath the faint scent of cordite and mingled with the thicker smell of blood was the smell of a cigar.

He took the flashlight from O'Reilly and trained it on the dirty snow against the curb. It had been trampled by everyone coming to this crime scene.

He crouched, and poked just a little, finding three fairly fresh cigarette butts.

As he stood, he said to the beat cops, "When the scene of the crime guys get here, make sure they take everything from the curb."

O'Reilly was watching him. The beat cops were frowning, but they nodded.

Bryce handed O'Reilly back his flashlight and head-ed down the street.

"You think he was smoking and tossing the butts out the window?" O'Reilly asked.

"Either that," Bryce said, "or he rolled his window down to talk to someone. And if someone was pointing a gun at him, he wouldn't have done it. This vehicle was armored. He had a better chance starting it up and driv-ing away than he did cooperating."

"If he wasn't smoking," O'Reilly said, "he knew his killer."

"Yeah," Bryce said. And he was pretty sure that was going to make his job a whole hell of a lot harder.

***

KENNEDY TOOK THE ELEVATOR up to the fifth floor of the Justice Department. He probably should have stayed home, but he simply couldn't. He needed to get into those files and he needed to do so before anyone else.

As he strode into the corridor he shared with the Di-rector of the FBI, he saw Helen Gandy hurry in the other direction. She looked like she had just come from the beauty salon. He had never seen her look anything less than completely put together but he was surprised by her perfect appearance on this night, after the news that her long-time boss was dead.

Kennedy tugged at the overcoat he'd put on over his favorite sweater. He hadn't taken the time to change or even comb his hair. He probably looked as tousled as he had in the days after Jack died.

Although, for the first time in three months, he felt like he had a purpose. He didn't know how long this feeling would last, or how long he wanted it to. But this death had given him an odd kind of hope that control was coming back into his world.

Haskell stood in front of the Director's office suite, arms crossed. The Director's suite was just down the corridor from the Attorney General's offices. It felt odd to go toward Hoover's domain instead of his own.

Haskell looked relieved when he saw Kennedy.

"Was that the dragon lady I just saw?" Kennedy asked.

"She wanted to get some personal effects from her office," Haskell said.

"Did you let her?"

"You said the orders were to secure it, so I have."

"Excellent." Kennedy glanced in both directions and saw no one. "Make sure your staff continues to protect the doors. I'm going inside."

"Sir?" Haskell raised his eyebrows.

"This may not be the right place," Kennedy said. "I'm worried that he moved everything to his house."

The lie came easily. Kennedy would have heard if Hoover had moved files to his own home. But Haskell didn't know that.

Haskell moved away from the door. It was unlocked. Two more agents stood inside, guarding the interior doors.

"Give me a minute, please, gentlemen," Kennedy said.

The men nodded and went outside.

Kennedy stopped and took a deep breath. He had been in Miss Gandy's office countless times, but he had never really looked at it. He'd always been staring at the door to Hoover's inner sanctum, waiting for it to open and the old man to come out.

That office was interesting. In the antechamber, Hoover had memorabilia and photographs from his major cases. He even had the plaster-of-paris death mask of John Dillinger on display. It was a ghastly thing, which made Kennedy think of the way that English kings used to keep severed heads on the entrance to London Bridge to warn traitors of their potential fate.

But this office had always looked like a waiting room to him. Nothing very special. The woman behind the desk was the focal point. Jack had been the one who nicknamed her the dragon lady and had even called her that to her face once, only with his trademark grin, so infectious that she hadn't made a sound or a grimace in protest.

Of course, she hadn't smiled back either.

Her desk was clear except for a blotter, a telephone, and a jar of pens. A typewriter sat on a credenza with paper stacked beside it.

But it wasn't the desk that interested him the most. It was the floor-to-ceiling filing cabinets and storage bins. He walked to them. Instead of the typical system— marked by letters of the alphabet—this one had numbers that were clearly part of a code.

He pulled open the nearest drawer, and found row after row of accordion files, each with its own number, and manila folders with the first number set followed by another. He cursed softly under his breath.

Of course the old dog wouldn't file his confidentials by name. He'd use a secret code. The old man liked nothing more than his secrets.

Still, Kennedy opened half a dozen drawers just to see if the system continued throughout. And it wasn't until he got to a bin near the corner of the desk that he found a file labeled "Obscene."

His hand shook as he pulled it out. Jack, for all his brilliance, had been sexually insatiable. Back when their brother Joe was still alive and no one ever thought Jack would be running for president, Jack had had an affair with a Danish émigré named Inga Arvad. Inga Binga, as Jack used to call her, was married to a man with ties to Hitler. She'd even met and liked Der Fuhrer, and had said so in print.

She'd been the target of FBI surveillance as a possible spy, and during that surveillance who should turn up in her bed but a young naval lieutentant whose father had once been Ambassador to England. The Ambassador, as he preferred to be called even by his sons, found out about the affair, told Jack in no uncertain terms to end it, and then to make sure he did by getting him assigned to a PT boat in the Pacific, as far from Inga Binga as possible.

Kennedy had always suspected that Hoover had leaked the information to the Ambassador, but he hadn't known for certain until Jack became President when Hoover told them. Hoover had been surveilling all of the Kennedy children at the Ambassador's request. He'd given Kennedy a list of scandalous items as a sample, and hoped that would control the president and his brother.

It might have controlled Jack, but Hoover hadn't known Kennedy very well. Kennedy had told Hoover that if any of this information made it into the press, then other things would appear in print as well, things like the strange FBI budget items for payments covering Hoover's visits to the track or the fact that Hoover made some interesting friends, mobster friends, when he was vacationing in Palm Beach.

It wasn't quite a Mexican stand-off—Jack was really afraid of the old man—but it gave Kennedy more power than any Attorney General had had over Hoover since the beginnings of the Roosevelt administration.

But now Kennedy needed those files, and he had a hunch Hoover would label them obscene.

Kennedy opened the file, and was shocked to see Richard Nixon's name on the sheets inside. Kennedy thumbed through quickly, not caring what dirt they'd found on that loser. Nixon couldn't win an election after his defeat in 1960. He'd even told the press after he lost a California race that they wouldn't have him to kick around any more.

Yet Hoover had kept the files, just to be safe.

That old bastard really and truly had known where all the bodies were buried. And it wouldn't be easy to find them.

Kennedy took a deep breath. He stood, shoved his hands in his pockets, and surveyed the walls of files. It would take days to search each folder. He didn't have days. He probably didn't have hours.

But he was Hoover's immediate supervisor, whether the old man had recognized it or not. Hoover answered to him. Which meant that the files belonged to the Justice Department, of which the FBI was only one small part.

He glanced at his watch. No one pounded on the door. He probably had until dawn before someone tried to stop him. If he was really lucky, no one would think of the files until mid-morning.

He went to the door and beckoned Haskell inside.

"We're taking the files to my office," he said.

"All of them, sir?"

"All of them. These first, then whatever is in Hoover's office, and then any other confidential files you can find."

Haskell looked up the wall as if he couldn't believe the command. "That'll take some time, sir."

"Not if you get a lot of people to help."

"Sir, I thought you wanted to keep this secret."

He did. But it wouldn't remain secret for long. So he had to control when the information got out—just like he had to control the information itself.

"Get this done as quickly as possible," he said.

Haskell nodded and turned the doorknob, but Kennedy stopped him before he went out.

"These are filed by code," he said. "Do you know where the key is?"

"I was told that Miss Gandy had the keys to everything from codes to offices," Haskell said.

Kennedy felt a shiver run through him. Knowing Hoover, he would have made sure he had the key to the Attorney General's office as well.

"Do you have any idea where she might have kept the code keys?" Kennedy asked.

"No," Haskell said. "I wasn't part of the need-to-know group. I already knew too much."

Kennedy nodded. He appreciated how much Haskell knew. It had gotten him this far.

"On your way out," Kennedy said, "call building maintenance and have them change all the locks in my office."

"Yes, sir." Haskell kept his hand on the doorknob. "Are you sure you want to do this, sir? Couldn't you just change the locks here? Wouldn't that secure everything for the President?"

"Everyone in Washington wants these files," Kennedy said. "They're going to come to this office suite. They won't think of mine."

"Until they heard that you moved everything."

Kennedy nodded. "And then they'll know how futile their quest really is."

***

THE FINAL CRIME SCENE was a mess. The bodies were already gone—probably inside the coroner's van that blocked the alley a few blocks back. It had taken Bryce nearly a half an hour to find someone who knew what the scene had looked like when the police had first arrived.

That someone was Officer Ralph Voight. He was tall and trim, with a pristine uniform despite the fact that he'd been on duty all night.

O'Reilly was the one who convinced him to talk with Bryce. Voight was the first to show the traditional animosity between the NYPD and the FBI, but that was because Voight didn't know who had died only a few blocks away.

Bryce had Voight walk him through the crime scene. The buildings on this street were boarded up, and the lights burned out. Broken glass littered the sidewalk—and it hadn't come from this particular crime. Rusted beer cans, half buried in the ice piles, cluttered each stoop like passed-out drunks.

"Okay," Voight said, using his flashlight as a pointer, "we come up on these two cars first."

The two sedans were parked against the curb, one behind the other. The sedans were too nice for the neighborhood—new, black, without a dent. Bryce recognized them as FBI issue—he had access to a sedan like that himself when he needed it.

He patted his pocket, was disgusted to realize he'd left his notebook at the apartment, and turned to O'Reilly. "You got paper? I need those plates."

O'Reilly nodded. He pulled out a notebook and wrote down the plate numbers.

"They just looked wrong," Voight was saying. "So we stopped, figuring maybe someone needed assistance."

He pointed the flashlight across the street. The squad had stopped directly across from the two cars.

"That's when we seen the first body."

He walked them to the middle of the street. This part of the city hadn't been plowed regularly and a layer of ice had built over the pavement. A large pool of blood had melted through that ice, leaving its edges reddish black and revealing the pavement below.

"The guy was face down, hands out like he'd tried to catch himself."

"Face gone?" Bryce asked, thinking maybe it was a head shot like the others.

"No. Turns out he was shot in the back."

Bryce glanced at O'Reilly, whose lips had thinned. This one was different. Because it was the first? Or because it was unrelated?

"We pull our weapons, scan to see if we see anyone else, which we don't. The door's open on the first sedan, but we didn't see anyone in the dome light. And we didn't see anyone obvious on the street, but it's really dark here and the flashlights don't reach far." Voight turned his light toward the block with the parked limousine, but neither the car nor the sidewalk was visible from this distance.

"So we go to the cars, careful now, and find the other body right there."

He flashed his light on the curb beside the door to the first sedan.

"This one's on his back and the door is open. We figure he was getting out when he got plugged. Then the other guy—maybe he was outside his car trying to help this guy with I don't know what, some car trouble or something, then his buddy gets hit, so he runs for cover across the street and gets nailed. End of story."

"Did you check to see if the cars start?" O'Reilly asked. Bryce nodded that was going to be his next question as well.

"I'm not supposed to touch the scene, sir," Voight said with some resentment. "We secured the area, figured everything was okay, then called it in."

"Did you hear the other shots?"

"No," Voight said. "I know we got three more up there, and you'd think I'd've heard the shooting if something happened, but I didn't. And as you can tell, it's damn quiet around here at night."

Bryce could tell. He didn't like the silence in the middle of the city. Neighborhoods that got quiet like this so close to dawn were usually among the worst. The early morning maintenance workers, and the delivery drivers stayed away whenever they could.

He peered in the sedan, then pulled the door open. The interior light went on, and there was blood all over the front seat and steering wheel. There were styrofoam coffee cups on both sides of the little rise between the seats. And the keys were in the ignition. Like all Bureau issue, the car was an automatic.

Carefully, so that he wouldn't disturb anything important in the scene, he turned the key. The sedan purred to life, sounding well-tuned just like it was supposed to.

"Check to see if there are other problems," Bryce said to O'Reilly. "A flat maybe."

Although Bryce knew there wouldn't be one. He shut off the ignition.

"You didn't see the interior light when you pulled up?" he asked Voight.

"Yeah, but it was dim," Voight said. "That's why I figured there was car problems. I figured they left the lights on so they could see."

Bryce nodded. He understood the assumption. He backed out of the sedan, then walked around it, shining his own flashlight at the hole in the ice, and then back at the first sedan.

Directly across.

He walked to the second sedan. Its interior was clean—no styrofoam cups, no wadded up food containers, no notebooks. Not even some tools hastily pulled to help the other drivers in need.

He let out a small sigh. He finally figured out what was bothering him.

"You find weapons on the two men?" he asked Voight.

"Yes, sir."

"Holstered?"

"The guy by the car. The other one had his in his right hand. We figured we just happened on the scene or someone would have taken the weapon."

Or not. People tended to hide for a while after shots were fired, particularly if they had nothing to do with the shootings but might get blamed anyway.

Bryce tried to open the passenger door on the second sedan, but it was locked. He walked around to the driver's door. Locked as well.

"No one looked inside this car?"

"No, sir. We figured crime scene would do it."

"But they haven't been here yet?" Bryce asked.

"It's the neighborhood, sir. Right there—" Voight aimed his flashlight at stairs heading down to a lower level "—is one of those men-only clubs, you know? The kind that you go to when you're…you know…looking for other men."

Bryce felt a flash of irritation. He'd been running into this all night. "Okay. What I'm hearing in a sideways way from every representative of the NYPD on this scene is that crimes in this neighborhood don't get investigated."

Voight sputtered. "They get investigated—"

"They get investigated," O'Reilly said, "enough to tell the families they probably want to back off. You heard Brunner. That's what most in the department call it. The rest of us, we call them lifestyle kills. And we get in trouble if we waste too many resources on them."

"Lovely," Bryce said dryly. His philosophy, which had gotten him in trouble with the Bureau more than once, was that all crimes deserved investigation, no matter how distasteful you found the victims. Which was why he kept getting moved, from communists to reviewing wire-taps to digging dirt on other agents.

And that was probably why he was here. He was expendable.

"Did you find car keys on either of the victims?" Bryce asked.

"No, sir," Voight said. "And I helped the coroner when he first arrived."

"Then start looking. See if they got dropped in the struggle."

Although Bryce doubted they had.

"I got something to jimmy the lock in my car," O'Reilly said.

Bryce nodded. Then he stood back, surveying the whole thing. He didn't like how he was thinking. It was making his heartburn grow worse.

But it was the only thing that made sense.

Agents worked HooverWatch in pairs. There were two dead agents and two cars. If the second sedan was back-up, there should have been four agents and two cars.

But it didn't look that way. It looked like someone had pulled up behind the HooverWatch vehicle, and got out, carefully locking the door.

Then he went to the door of the HooverWatch car. The driver had got out to talk to him, and the new guy shot him.

At that point, the second HooverWatch agent was an easy target. He scrambled out of the car, grabbed his own weapon, and headed across the street—maybe shooting as he went. The shooter got him, and then casually walked up the street to the limo, which he had to know was there even though he couldn't see it.

As he approached the limo, the limo driver lowered his window. He would have recognized the approaching man, and thought he was going to report on the danger.

Instead, the man shot him, then went to lie in wait for Hoover and Tolson.

Bryce shivered. It would have happened very fast, and long before the beat cops showed up.

The guy in the street had time to bleed out. The limo driver couldn't warn his boss. And the beat cops hadn't heard the shots in the alley, which they would have on such a quiet night.

O'Reilly brought the jimmy, shoved it into the space between the window and the lock, and flipped the lock up with a single movement. Then he opened the door.

No keys in the ignition.

Bryce flipped open the glovebox. Nothing inside but the vehicle registration. Which, as he expected, identified it as an FBI vehicle.

The shooter had planned to come back. He'd planned to drive away in this car. But he got delayed. And by the time he got here, the two beat cops were on scene. He couldn't get his car.

He had to improvise. So he probably walked away or took the subway, hoping the cops would think the extra car belonged to one of the victims.

And that was his mistake.

"How come you guys were here in the middle of the night?" Bryce asked Voight.

Voight swallowed. It was the first sign of nervousness he'd shown. "This is part of our beat."

"But?" Bryce asked.

Voight looked away. "We're supposed to go up Central Park West."

"And you don't."

"Yeah, we do. Just not every time."

"Because?"

"Because I figure, you know, when the bars let out, we could, you know, let our presence be known."

"Prevent a lifestyle kill."

"Yes, sir."

"And you care about this because…?"

"Everyone should," Voight snapped. "Serve and protect, right, sir?"

Voight was touchy. He thought Bryce was accusing him of protecting the lifestyle because he lived it.

"Does your partner like this drive?" Bryce asked.

"He complains, sir, but he lets me do it."

"Have you stopped any crimes?"

"Broken up a few fights," Voight said.

"But not something like this."

"No, sir."

"You don't patrol every night, do you, Voight?"

"No, sir. We get different regions different nights."

"Do you think our killer would have thought that this street was unprotected?"

"It usually is, sir."

O'Reilly was frowning, but not at Voight. At Bryce. "You think this was planned?" O'Reilly asked.

Bryce didn't answer. This was a Bureau matter, and he wasn't sure how the Bureau would handle it.

But he did think the killing was planned. And he had a hunch it would be easy to solve because of the abandoned sedan.

And that abandoned sedan bothered him more than he wanted to admit. Because the presence of that sedan meant only one thing: that the person who had shot all five FBI agents was—almost without a doubt—an FBI agent himself.

***

KENNEDY LOOKED AT THE BINS and the filing cabinets stacked around his office and allowed himself one moment to feel overwhelmed. People ribbed him about the office; he had taken the reception area and made it his, rather than use the standard size office in the back.

As a result, his office was as long as a football field, with stunning windows along the walls. The watercolors painted by his children had been covered by the cabinets. His furniture was pushed aside to make room for the bins, and for the first time, this space felt small.

He put his hands on his hips and wondered how to begin.

Since six agents began moving the filing cabinets across the corridor more than an hour ago, Kennedy had received five phone calls from LBJ's chief of staff. Kennedy hadn't taken one of them. The last had been a direct order to come to the Oval Office.

Kennedy ignored it.

He also ignored the ringing telephone—the White House line—and the messages his own assistant (called in after a short night's sleep) had been bringing to him.

Helen Gandy stood in the corridor, arms crossed, her purse hanging off her wrist, and watching with deep disapproval. Haskell was trying to find out if there were remaining files and where they were. But Kennedy had found the one thing he was looking for: the key.

It was in a large, innocuous index file box inside the lowest drawer of Helen Gandy's desk. Kennedy had brought it into his office and was thumbing through it, hoping to understand it before he got interrupted again.

A man from building maintenance had changed the lock on the door leading into the interior offices, and was working on the main doors now that the files were all inside. Kennedy figured he'd have his own office secure by seven a.m.

Then he heard a rustling in the hallway, a lot of startled, "Mr. President, sir!" followed by official, "Make way for the President," and instinctively he turned toward the door. The maintenance man was leaning out of it, the door knob loose in his hand.

"Where the fuck is that bastard?" Lyndon Baines Johnson's voice echoed from the corridor. "Doesn't anyone in this building have balls enough to tell him that he works for me?"

Even though the question was rhetorical, someone tried to answer. Kennedy heard something about "your orders, sir."

"Horseshit!" Then LBJ stood in the doorway. Two secret service agents flanked him. He motioned with one hand at the maintenance man. "I suggest you get out."

The man didn't have to be told twice. He scurried away, still carrying the doorknob. LBJ came inside alone, pushed the door closed, then grimaced as it popped back open. He grabbed a chair and set it in front of the door, then glared at Kennedy.

The glare was effective in that hang-dog face, despite LBJ's attire. He wore a plaid silk pajama top stuffed into a pair of suitpants, finished with dress shoes and no socks. His hair—what remained of it—hadn't been Brilcremed down like usual, and stood up on the sides and the back.

"I get a phone call from some weasel underling of that Old Cocksucker, informing me that he's dead, and you're stealing from his tomb. I try to contact you, find out that you are indeed removing files from the Director's office, and that you won't take my calls. Now, I should've sent one of my boys over here, but I figured they're still walking on tip-toe around you because you're in fucking mourning, and this don't require tip-toe. Especially since you got to be wondering about now what the hell you did to deserve all of this."

"Deserve what?" Kennedy had expected LBJ's anger, but he hadn't expected it so soon. He also hadn't expected it here, in his office, instead of in the Oval Office a day or so later.

"Well, there's only two things that tie J. Edgar and your brother. The first is that someone was gunning for them and succeeded. The second is that they went after the mob on your bidding. There's a lot of shit running around here that says your brother's shooting was a mob hit, and I know personally that J. Edgar was doing his best to make it seem like that Oswald character acted alone. But now Edgar is dead and Jack is dead and the only tie they have is the way they kow-towed to your stupid prosecution of the men that got your brother elected."

Kennedy felt lightheaded. He hadn't even thought that the deaths of his brother and J. Edgar were connected. But LBJ had a point. Maybe there was a conspiracy to kill government officials. Maybe the mob was showing its power. He'd had warning.

Hell, he'd had suspicions. He hadn't let himself look at any of the evidence in his brother's assassination, not after he secured the body and prevented a disastrous autopsy in Texas. If those doctors at Parkland had done their job, they would've seen just how advanced Jack's Addison's disease was. The best kept secret of the Kennedy Administration—an administration full of secrets—was how close Jack was to incapacitation and death.

Kennedy clutched the file box. But LBJ knew that. He knew a lot of the secrets—had even promised to keep a few of them. And he wanted the files as badly as Kennedy did.

There had to be a lot in here on LBJ too. Not just the women, which was something he had in common with Jack, but other things, from his days in Congress.

"From what I heard," Kennedy said, making certain his voice was calm even though he wasn't, "all they know is someone shot Hoover. Did you get more details than that? Something that mentions organized crime in particular?"

"I'm sure it'll come out," LBJ said.

"You're sure that saying such things would upset me," Kennedy said. "You're after the files."

"Damn straight," LBJ said. "I'm the head of this government. Those files are mine."

"You're the head of this government for another year. Next January, someone'll take the oath of office and it might not be you. Do you really want to claim these in the name of the presidency? Because you might be handing them over to Goldwater come January."

LBJ blanched.

Someone knocked on the door, and startled both men. Kennedy frowned. He couldn't think of anyone who would have enough nerve to interrupt him when he was getting shouted at by LBJ. But someone had.

LBJ pulled the door open. Helen Gandy stood there.

"You boys can be heard in the hallway," she said, sweeping in as if the leader of the free world wasn't holding the door for her. "And it's embarrassing. It was precisely this kind of thing the Director hoped to avoid."

Then she nodded at LBJ. Kennedy watched her. The dragon lady. Jack, as usual, had been right with his jibes. Only the dragon lady would walk in here as if she were the most important person in the room.

"Mr. President," she said, "these files are the Director's personal business. He wanted me to take care of them, and get them out of the office, where they do not belong."

"Personal files, Miss Gandy?" LBJ asked. "These are his secret files."

"If they were secret, Mr. President, then you wouldn't be here. Mr. Hoover kept his secrets."

Mr. Hoover used his secrets, Kennedy thought, but didn't say.

"These are just his confidential files," Miss Gandy was saying. "Let me take care of them and they won't be here to tempt anyone. That's what the Director wanted."

"These are government property," LBJ said with a sly look at Kennedy. For the first time, Kennedy realized his Goldwater argument had gotten through. "They belong here. I do thank you for your time and concern, though, ma'am."

Then he gave her a courtly little bow, put his hand on the small of her back, and propelled her out of the room.

Despite himself Kennedy was impressed. He'd never seen anyone handle the dragon lady that efficiently before.

LBJ grabbed one of the cabinets and slid it in front of the door he had just closed. Kennedy had forgotten how strong the man was. He had invited Kennedy down to his Texas ranch before the election, trying to find out what Kennedy was made of, and instead, Kennedy had realized just what LBJ was made of—strength, not bluster, brains *and* brawn.

He'd do well to remember that.

"All right," LBJ said as he turned around. "Here's what I'm gonna offer. You can have your family's files. You can watch while we search for them and you can have everything. Just give me the rest."

Kennedy raised his eyebrows. He hadn't felt this alive since November. "No."

"I can fire your ass in five minutes, put someone else in this fancy office, and then you can't do a goddamn thing," LBJ said. "I'm being kind."

"There's historical precedent for a cabinet member barricading himself in his office after he got fired," Kennedy said. "Seems to me it happened to a previous president named Johnson. While I'm barricaded in, I'll just go through the files and find out everything I need to know."

LBJ crossed his arms.

It was a stand-off and neither of them had a good play. They only had a guess as to what was in those files—not just theirs but all of the others as well. They did know that whatever was in those files had given Hoover enough power to last in the office for more than forty years.

The files had brought down presidents. They could bring down congressmen, supreme court justices, and maybe even the current president. In that way, Helen Gandy was right.

The best solution was to destroy everything.

Only Kennedy wouldn't. Just like he knew LBJ wouldn't. There was too much history here, too much knowledge.

And too much power.

"These are our files," Kennedy said after a moment, although the word "our" galled him, "yours and mine. Right now we control them."

LBJ nodded, almost imperceptivity. "What do you want?"

What did he want? To be left alone? To have his family left alone? At midnight, he might have said that. But now, his old self was reasserting itself. He felt like the man who had gone after the corrupt leaders of the Teamsters, not the man who had accidentally gotten his brother murdered.

Besides, there might be things in that file that could head off other problems in the future. Other murders. Other manipulations.

He needed a bullet-proof position. LBJ was right: the Attorney General could be fired. But there was one position, constitutionally, that the president couldn't touch.

"I want to be your Vice President," Kennedy said. "And in 1972, when you can't run again, I want your endorsement. I want you to back me for the nomination."

LBJ swallowed hard. Color suffused his face and for a moment, Kennedy thought he was going to shout again.

But he didn't.

Instead he said, "And what happens if we don't win?"

"We move these to a location of our choosing. And we do it with trusted associates. We get this stuff out of here."

LBJ glanced at the door. He was clearly thinking of what Helen Gandy had said, how it was better to be rid of all of this than it was to have it corrupting the office, endangering everyone.

But if LBJ and Kennedy controlled the entire cache, they also controlled their own files. LBJ could destroy his and Kennedy could preserve his family's legacy.

If it weren't for the fact that LBJ hated him almost as much as Kennedy hated LBJ, the decision would be easy.

"You'd trust me to a gentleman's agreement?" LBJ asked, not disguising the sarcasm in his tone. He knew Kennedy thought he was too uncouth to ever be considered a gentleman.

"You know where your interests lie. Just like I do," Kennedy said. "If we don't let Miss Gandy have the files, then this is the only choice."

LBJ sighed. "I hoped to be rid of the Kennedys by inauguration day."

"And what if I planned to run against you?" Kennedy asked, even though he knew he wouldn't. Already the party stalwarts had been approaching him about a 1964 presidential bid, and he had put them off. He had been too shaky, too emotionally fragile.

He didn't feel fragile now.

LBJ didn't answer that question. Instead, he said, "You can be an incautious asshole. Why should I trust you?"

"Because I saved Jack's ass more times than you can count," Kennedy said. "I'm saving yours too."

"How do you figure?" LBJ asked.

"Your fear of those files brought you to me, Mr. President." Kennedy put an emphasis on the title, which he usually avoided using around LBJ. "If I barricade myself in here, I'll have the keys to the kingdom and no qualms about letting the information free when I go free. If you work with me, your secrets remain just secrets."

"You're a son of bitch, you know that?" LBJ asked.

Kennedy nodded. "The hell of it is you are too or you wouldn't've brought up Jack's death before we knew what really happened to Hoover. So let's control the presidency for the next sixteen years. By then the information in these files will probably be worthless."

LBJ stared at him. It took Kennedy a minute to realize that although he'd won the argument, he wouldn't get an agreement from LBJ, not if Kennedy didn't make the first move.

Kennedy held out his hand. "Deal?"

LBJ stared at Kennedy's extended hand for a long moment before taking it in his own big clammy one.

"You goddamn son of a bitch," LBJ said. "You've got a deal."

***

IT TOOK BRYCE ONLY ONE PHONE CALL. The guy who ran the motorpool told him who checked out the sedan without asking why Bryce want to know. And Bryce, as he leaned in the cold telephone booth half a block from the first crime scene, instantly understood what had happened and why.

The agent who checked out the sedan was Walter Cain. He should've been on extended leave. Bryce had recommended it after he had told Cain that his ex-fiancé had tried to commit suicide. On getting the news, Cain had just had that look, that blank, my-life-is-over look.

And it had scared Bryce. Scared him enough that he asked Cain be put on indefinite leave. How long ago had that been? Less than twelve hours.

More than enough time to get rid of the morals police—the one man who made all the rules at the FBI. The man who had no morals himself.

J. Edgar Hoover.

Bryce had spent the past week studying Cain's file. Cain had had HooverWatch off and on throughout the past year. Cain knew the procedure, and he knew how to thwart it.

He'd killed five agents.

Because no one would listen to Bryce about that vacant look in Cain's eye.

Bryce let himself out of the phone booth. He walked back to the coroner's van. If he didn't have back up by now, he'd call for some all over again. They couldn't leave him hanging on this. They had to let him know, if nothing else, what to do with the Director's body.

But he needn't've worried. When he got back to the alley, he saw five more sedans, all FBI issue. And as he stepped into the alley proper, the first person he saw was his boss, crouching over Hoover's corpse.

"I thought I told you to secure the scene," said the SAC for the District of New York, Eugene Hart. "In fact, I ordered you to do it."

"The scene extends over six blocks. I'm just one guy," Bryce said.

Hart walked over to him. He looked tired.

"I need to speak to you," Bryce said. He walked Hart back to the two sedans, explained what he'd learned, and watched Hart's face.

The man flinched, then, to Bryce's surprise, put his hand on Bryce's shoulder. "It's good work."

Bryce didn't thank him. He was worried that Hart hadn't asked any questions. "I'd heard Cain bitch more than once about Hoover setting the moral values for the office. And with what happened this week—"

"I know." Hart squeezed his shoulder. "We'll take care of it."

Bryce turned so quickly that he made Hart lose his grip. "You're going to cover it up."

Hart closed his eyes.

"You weren't hanging me out to dry. You were trying to figure out how to handle this. Son of a bitch. And you're going to let Cain walk."

"He won't walk," Hart said. "He'll just…be guilty of something else."

"You can't cover this up. It's too important. So soon after President Kennedy—"

"That's precisely why we're going to handle it," Hart said. "We don't want a panic."

"And you don't want anyone to know where Hoover and Tolson were found. What're you going to say? That they died of natural causes in their beds? Their *separate* beds?"

"It's not your concern," Hart said. "You've done well for us. You'll be rewarded."

"If I keep my mouth shut."

Hart sighed. He didn't seem to have the energy to glare. "I don't honestly care. I'm glad to have the old man gone. But I'm not in charge of this. We've got orders now, and everything'll get taken care of at a much higher level than either you or me.

You should be grateful for that."

Bryce supposed he should be. It took the political pressure off him. It also took the personal pressure off.

But he couldn't help feeling if someone had listened to him before, if someone had paid attention, then none of this would have happened.

No one cared that an FBI agent was going to marry a former prostitute. If the Bureau knew—and it did, then not even the KGB could use that as blackmail.

It was all about appearances. It would always be about appearances. Hoover had designed a damn booklet about appearances, and it hadn't stopped him from getting shot in a back alley after a party he would never admit attending.

Hoover had been so worried about people using secrets against each other, he hadn't even realized how his own secrets could be used against him.

Bryce looked at Hart. They were both tired. It had been a long night. And it would be an even longer few weeks for Hart. Bryce would get some don't-tell promotion and he'd stay there for as long as he had to. He had to make sure that Cain got prosecuted for something, that he paid for five deaths.

Then Bryce would resign.

He didn't need the Bureau, any more than he had needed Mary, his own pre-approved wife. Maybe he'd talk to O'Reilly, see if he could put in a good word with the NYPD. At least the NYPD occasionally investigated cases.

If they happened in the right neighborhood.

To the right people.

Bryce shoved his hands in his pockets and walked back to his apartment. Hart didn't try to stop him. They both knew Bryce's work on this case was done. He wouldn't even have to write a report.

In fact, he didn't dare write a report, didn't dare put any of this on paper where someone else might discover it. The wrong someone. Someone who didn't care about handling and the proper information.

Someone who would use that information to his own benefit.

Like the Director had.

For more than forty-five years.

Bryce shook the thought off. It wasn't his concern. He no longer had concerns. Except getting a good night's sleep.

And somehow he knew that he wouldn't get one of those for a long, long time.

About the Author

International bestselling writer Kristine Kathryn Rusch has published fiction in every genre. She has been nominated for three Edgar Awards, two Shamus Awards, and an Anthony Award. She has won the *Ellery Queen* Reader's Choice Award twice. She has also published award-winning mystery novels under the name Kris Nelscott. For more about her work, go to kristinekathrynrusch.com.

Also by
Kristine Kathryn Rusch

The Retrieval Artist Series:

The Disappeared
Extremes
Consequences
Buried Deep
Paloma
Recovery Man
Duplicate Effort
Anniversary Day
Blowback

The Smokey Dalton Series (as Kris Nelscott):

A Dangerous Road
Smoke-Filled Rooms
Thin Walls
Stone Cribs
War at Home
Days of Rage

WMG
Publishing